COLD CASE

COLD CASE

JULIA PLATT LEONARD

ALADDIN
NEW YORK LONDON TORONTO SYDNEY NEW DELHI

ALADDIN
An imprint of Simon & Schuster Children's Publishing Division
1230 Avenue of the Americas, New York, NY 10020
First Aladdin paperback edition May 2012
Copyright © 2011 by Julia Platt Leonard
All rights reserved, including the right of reproduction in whole or in part in any form.
Aladdin is a trademark of Simon & Schuster, Inc.,
and related logo is a registered trademark of Simon & Schuster, Inc.
Also available in an Aladdin hardcover edition.
For information about special discounts for bulk purchases,
please contact Simon & Schuster Special Sales at 1-866-506-1949
or business@simonandschuster.com. The Simon & Schuster Speakers Bureau
can bring authors to your live event. For more information or to book an event
contact the Simon & Schuster Speakers Bureau at 1-866-248-3049
or visit our website at www.simonspeakers.com.
The text of this book was set in Adobe Caslon.
Manufactured in the United States of America 0312 OFF
10 9 8 7 6 5 4 3 2 1
The Library of Congress has cataloged the hardcover edition as follows:
Cold case / by Julia Platt Leonard—1st Aladdin hardcover ed.
p. cm.
Summary: When thirteen-year-old Oz Keiller finds a dead body in his family's Santa Fe, New Mexico, restaurant, he is determined to solve the mystery in which his older brother is implicated, but which also involves their long-dead father, who was accused of being a spy.
[1. Mystery and detective stories 2. Murder—Fiction. 3. Brothers—Fiction.
4. Restaurants—Fiction. 5. Spies—Fiction. 6. Family life—New Mexico—Fiction.
7. Santa Fe (N.M.)—Fiction] 1. Title
PZ7.L5473 Col 2011
[Fic] —dc22
2010041854
ISBN 978-1-4424-2009-0 (hc)
ISBN 978-1-4424-2010-6 (pbk)
ISBN 978-1-4424-2750-1 (eBook)

For Zach

SATURDAY

CHAPTER 1

BA-BA-BA. I swatted at the alarm clock. *BA-BA-BA.* Where was the snooze button? I fumbled for the light and knocked over a glass of water. By the time I got the light on, and alarm off, water was everywhere. I picked up Dave's copy of *Making of a Cook* and dried it off on my pillowcase.

Great. Six o'clock a.m. and the day was off to a bad start.

It wasn't going to get any better, either. I slid out of bed and fished a pair of jeans and a crumpled T-shirt from underneath a chair and yanked them on. Thanks to Dave—he's my older brother—I got to spend Saturday morning cleaning greasy exhaust hoods and scrubbing down counters. Oh yeah, and stock-take . . . a riveting job where I counted how much we had of every ingredient in the kitchen. Fascinating, *not*.

He didn't even care that school had just started and I had homework to do. He gave me a big lecture last night. "Oz, this is the only way you'll ever learn the business. All the great chefs start this way." And then—this is the killer—"Trust me, I'm doing you a favor." Thanks, Dave.

I splashed cold water on my face and brushed my teeth. I caught a glimpse of my face in the mirror and squinted at my reflection. Maybe we weren't really brothers. He had blond hair and blue eyes. Me? Brown hair, brown eyes, and freckles. I could hope.

I walked down the hall past his bedroom. Totally silent. He got to sleep in while I worked. Okay, so we were short staffed. And he was the head chef. And he was twelve years older than me. I got all that. But still, he treated me like I was his personal slave.

It was worse because Mom wasn't here. She'd been in France for almost a week. She flew out as soon as we got the call that Gran had had a stroke. Mom was barely out of the driveway before Dave put on his serious face and said, "Oz, we all have to pitch in." I think it was just another excuse to hassle me.

I put on my backpack and grabbed my bike from the front porch. I was almost out the driveway before I realized something was weird. Dave's car wasn't there. I hadn't heard him come in last night, but I was so exhausted that wasn't surprising. A sick thought raced through my mind. What if Dave was already at work? What if he'd gone in early so he could keep an eye on me? Great. That was all I needed.

I zoomed down Garcia, took a right onto Acequia Madre and a left at Delgado. Piñon smoke wafted out of a chimney, a smell of pine and cumin that reminded me of Christmas. I sucked in a deep breath. Except for a couple of dogs howling, it was just me.

At Canyon Road I took a right. The galleries were closed, waiting for the next wave of art-crazed tourists. We got our fair share of tourists at Chez Isabelle—most of the local businesses depended on them—but also lots of locals.

When I hit the parking lot I slowed down. Suddenly it was pitch black. Weird. I could barely see the restaurant across the lot. It wasn't a big deal. I spent more time at Chez Isabelle than I did at home and knew my way around blindfolded, but still . . .

I coasted across the lot and leaned my bike against

the wall. I felt my way to the door. Glass crunched underneath my shoes. That was it. The light over the back door was out. Probably Razor and JoJo playing hoops again. "Excellent," I muttered. "One more thing to clean up."

I shifted my backpack onto one shoulder and dug in the zipper pocket for my key. I fumbled around until I found the lock. The key slipped in but the lock didn't turn. It wasn't locked. Impossible. Dave closed last night, didn't he? He never forgot anything, especially something like locking up. I got this creepy feeling. I knew he'd been in a foul mood last night, distracted, like something was really bugging him, but forget to lock up?

I stood in the doorway, trying to figure out what to do. "Hello?" I called out. "Dave, you there?"

No one answered. I told myself there was nothing to worry about. I tried to ignore the butterflies in my stomach. I stepped through the doorway. Total darkness. It took a second for my eyes to adjust. I smelled cooking grease and bleach and something else . . . something different . . . what was it? It was like rust or . . .

I ran my hand along the wall to my right, found the light switch, and gave it a flick. As soon as the fluorescent lights sputtered on I felt better.

But then I saw it. Blood. The prep table—the stainless-steel one we used for pastry—was covered in blood. My stomach heaved. *Don't puke.* It *was* blood, wasn't it? I swallowed hard. There was more on the floor in front of the table. I glanced up. Droplets peppered the ceiling. I swallowed again.

I grabbed my cell and started to punch in the speed dial for Dave. I stopped. Dave would ask me a load of questions. I didn't have any answers. *Figure out what's going on, then call Dave.* I slipped the phone back in my pocket.

I glanced around at the rest of the room. Nothing moved, nothing missing as far as I could tell. Everything else looked normal. I took a step toward the table. A trail of blood led from the table in the center of the room to the walk-in fridge on the right-hand wall. Then it stopped. I edged over toward the fridge, trying not to step in the blood. It was no good. It squelched underneath my sneakers. I looked down. I'd left a bloody footprint on the floor.

I rested my hand on the cold stainless-steel door, trying to get my heart to stop racing. Maybe this was a practical joke. Something Razor thought up. He was our sous-chef, the second-in-command to Dave. Maybe I'd open up the door and he'd be in there with a couple of the other guys in hysterics.

I gripped the stainless-steel handle of the fridge. I took a deep breath and pulled. A blast of cold air hit me. That's when I saw him. It wasn't Razor or any of the guys from work. It was a man slumped against the back wall of the walk-in. There was a small trickle of blood on his forehead. But his shirt . . . his shirt was covered in blood. He didn't move. Dead. But his eyes . . . they were wide open and staring straight at me.

CHAPTER II

I stared at the man. He was dead, wasn't he? A voice inside my head kicked in: Find out. Make sure.

I propped a crate against the walk-in door to keep it open. I took a step, then another, and knelt down next to him. His chest wasn't moving. *I can't do this*, I thought. *You have to. Focus.* I pressed two fingers to his throat. He was cold—really cold. His skin was clammy. It felt like . . . I yanked my fingers back. No pulse. Nothing.

My heart raced. I couldn't get enough air. *Stay calm.* I forced myself to sit back on my heels and breathe slowly. *Think.* Who was he? What was he doing here? Chubby white guy. Button-down, chinos, and those tassel loafers middle-aged guys wear. He looked like Joe Tourist. You see them every day in Santa Fe. But there was something familiar about him. What was it?

I had to get out of there. I tried to stand, but I was dizzy. I grabbed the shelf next to me to get my balance. That's when I saw it. In his shirt pocket. A piece of paper. I squatted back down and looked closer. I knew I shouldn't touch it, but I couldn't help it. I eased the paper out of his pocket. My hands shook as I unfolded it.

```
D. Keiller

Fri night-midnight.

Use back door.
```

D. Keiller? *Dave?* Dave knew this guy? He met him last night? I was about to read it again when I heard a noise.

Click.

I whirled around. The back door . . . someone just opened the door. Heels hit the tile floor softly, slowly, barely making a sound. They were coming straight toward me. I didn't think. I shoved the note in my pocket. I stood up and pressed myself against the walk-in shelves.

Hide. Where? Nowhere to hide. I was stuck in a cold

metal box with nowhere to go except back out into the kitchen. But I had to do something, and fast.

The footsteps stopped. Silence. Where was he? What was he doing? I had to run for it. No choice. Sprint to the hall. Head for the front door.

I ran out of the walk-in and back into the kitchen. But I didn't make it far. The floor was slippery and I hit a pool of blood and skidded. I tried to get my balance, keep running, but a hand grabbed my arm. I spun around.

"Don't move," he said. I jerked my arm back, but his grip was too tight. The room was so bright, and lights were flashing behind him. I couldn't think, couldn't focus.

"Settle down. You're not going anywhere."

He was right. I stopped struggling, and he loosened his grip. He called out over his shoulder to someone in the parking lot. While he wasn't looking, I checked him out. Big. Built like a linebacker. Khaki-colored shirt, pants, badge . . . Badge? *Police?* I almost laughed. He was a cop. He was a good guy. It was okay. My body relaxed. Everything was going to be okay.

He caught me staring at him, with that stupid grin on my face. Only problem was that he wasn't smiling. "You want to tell me what's going on here?" he asked. He gave me that "You're busted" look cops do when they talk to teenagers. My smile dried up.

There was blood on the floor and a dead man in the walk-in, and a cop had caught me trying to run away. It wasn't okay, was it? Not by a long shot.

CHAPTER III

The weirdest thing? I was sure I knew the dead man. Not like I knew Dave or Mom, but I'd definitely seen him before. I tried to figure it out, but it was no good. It was like my brain had a computer virus. No matter how hard I tried, I couldn't get past this endless loop of blood, the body, the walk-in. Everything else was shut down—blue screen, fatal error.

Luckily, none of the cops asked me if I knew him. Actually, they didn't ask me anything. The first cop shoved me into the back of his cruiser, cracked the window like I was a dog, and told me to wait. Wait for what? I sat there while more police showed up, then forensics guys in one-piece coveralls and boots, like on television. What were they doing? And where was Dave?

I'd told them Mom was in France and gave them our home phone number, then Dave's cell. They tried both but no answer. The cop shot me a look like it was my fault they couldn't find Dave. My face got hot and I mumbled, "Probably in the shower." What an idiot.

Then they forgot about me. I thought about calling Rusty—she's my best friend—just so I could talk to someone. But then I checked my watch. Bad idea. It was way too early for Rusty. I glanced out the window. No one seemed to care what I did, so I texted Dave. WHERE ARE U???

"No phones." I dropped the phone in my lap like I'd touched a hot burner. I hadn't even heard this guy walk up. He stared at me through the window. Clean-shaven head and solid, like he did a lot of weights. He had on a striped short-sleeved shirt and tie, no jacket.

"Detective Suarez," he introduced himself. "Why don't you step outside so I can ask you a couple of questions?" He smiled, but it wasn't an "I'm your friend" kind of smile. It was a "Get your butt out of the car" smile. So I got out of the car.

"Want to tell me what happened?" he said. He crossed his arms and stared at me. His eyes were dark and didn't blink. He wasn't much taller than me, but everything about him was big, and he had "Don't mess with me" written all over him. I got the message.

"Well, I got here . . ." My voice cracked. I swallowed.

"Back up," he interrupted. "You always come to work this early?"

"No . . . I mean, sometimes I do, but not usually. Dave—"

"That's your brother?"

"Yeah, my brother. He told me to come in early. Do the big clean. Get things ready for weekend service . . ." My voice petered out. Suarez just looked at me. This wasn't going well. "See, we're . . ."

A car door slammed shut and footsteps pounded across the lot. We both looked up. It was Dave. He came running over.

"What's going on?" He looked quickly from me to Suarez and back again. His eyes flashed at me. "Well? What've you done now?" he demanded.

"*Me*? I haven't done anything."

Dave started to say something but stopped. What was wrong with him? He looked like he'd slept in his clothes. He was a wreck, and Dave's never a wreck. I caught Suarez watching us. He didn't say anything, just tilted his head for a second and nodded like he'd figured something out. Finally he spoke to Dave.

"Are you Mr. Keiller?"

"Yes. What's this about?"

"There's been a murder, Mr. Keiller. At your restaurant."

"What . . . ?" Dave shook his head. "You're joking." Dave looked at me, and I nodded slowly.

"It's true, Mr. Keiller. Your brother found a dead body inside the walk-in refrigerator."

Dave spun back toward me. "You what? Why didn't you call me?"

Suarez jumped in before I could answer. "We received an anonymous 911 call, Mr. Keiller. When we arrived, we tried you at home and on your cell, but you didn't answer. Do you mind telling me where you were?"

Dave paused. It was just for a second, but it was long enough. "Out. Driving," he said. "I . . . I couldn't sleep."

I thought about his car missing from the driveway this morning. He had been out, but where?

Dave tried to run his hand through his hair, but a gauze bandage was wrapped tightly around his knuckles and across his palm. Tiny dots of blood had soaked through the bandage. I'd left the restaurant around nine thirty last night. When I left, Dave was okay. What happened after I went home?

"Dave . . . your hand . . . ?"

Dave looked at me blankly, like he had no clue what I was talking about.

"Your hand, Mr. Keiller. It's bleeding. Looks like you hurt yourself," said Suarez. His voice was flat, but I could tell he was making a mental note about Dave's injury.

"It's nothing. I cut myself last night. That's all." Dave shoved his injured hand in his pocket. "I still don't understand what's going on," he said, trying to change the subject. "What happened? Who was killed?" He looked at me. His eyes were big. "It wasn't one of the guys, was it?"

I shook my head. "No . . ." I stopped. But who was Dead Guy? I had that feeling again. I was sure I'd seen him before.

Dave clenched his jaw and shook his head. "What a mess," he muttered. I knew what he was thinking. It wouldn't take long for word to get out that there had been a murder at Chez Isabelle. *Dead body + restaurant = bad for business.* Dave looked over at Detective Suarez. He tried to sound casual, but I could hear the panic creeping in.

"Any idea how long this is going to take?" Dave said. "I mean, to wrap things up."

"As long as it takes, Mr. Keiller."

"It's just . . . I'm sure you can understand. I've got a restaurant to run . . . a job to do." Dave tried to smile, but it came across as patronizing. Bad idea.

"I've got a job to do too, Mr. Keiller. Someone was murdered. Your restaurant is closed until we figure out what happened."

Dave started to say something but stopped. It wasn't like Suarez was going to change his mind, so why bother? The problem was that Dave liked to be in charge. Now he wasn't, and he didn't like it. Besides, he didn't want to believe what had happened. But then, he hadn't seen the body like I had. He hadn't seen the look on the man's face, the way Dead Guy's eyes stared. But I had. I'd seen him.

Something snapped. I *had* seen Dead Guy before. At Chez Isabelle. He'd eaten dinner here last night. I racked my brain and tried to remember something, anything. Where had Dead Guy sat? What did he eat? Was he alone? But it didn't really matter, did it? Dead Guy was dead. Now Chez Isabelle was closed. And if we didn't find out what happened soon, Chez Isabelle would be dead too.

CHAPTER IV

"Recognize this man?" Suarez slid a grainy black-and-white photograph across the table to Dave and me. The detective sat on one side; we were on the other. We'd only been in the interview room for five minutes, but I couldn't wait to get out of there.

The problem was I hadn't told Dave that Dead Guy was a customer . . . or ex-customer. I knew I should have—I wanted to—but the cops never left us alone for a minute. Then Suarez "invited" us back to the police station. What were we going to do? Say no?

I stared at the photo. It looked like someone had blown up the original about ten times, but it was definitely Dead Guy.

Dave glanced down at Dead Guy's pic. As soon as he did, his eyes bugged out and a wave of shock washed over his face. He struggled to get a grip, but his face spelled panic. I knew what it was: He recognized Dead Guy too.

I darted a quick look at Suarez. His head was down and he was leafing through a manila file folder. "Mr. Keiller, I asked you if you recognized this man."

"Sorry, I was just thinking," said Dave. "I . . . it's hard to tell. It's not a great picture, is it?" What was Dave doing? Of course he recognized the picture.

Suarez looked up from the folder and stared at Dave. The panic was gone—almost. Dave met Suarez's stare and said, "Mind telling me what's going on?"

Suarez tapped the photo with a paper clip. "This is the man we found murdered in your restaurant. He had a head contusion and died of multiple stab wounds. According to the ME, he was killed early this morning, probably before two a.m."

"No, that can't be," stammered Dave. The blood had drained from his face.

My chest tightened. The note I found in Dead Guy's pocket said he was meeting Dave at midnight. Dave and Dead Guy alone in the restaurant. *Dave, what have you done?*

"Can you tell me where you were early this morning?" Suarez asked.

"I—I told you," said Dave. "I was at home. Asleep. I woke up and couldn't go back to sleep, so I went for a drive. End of story."

"The problem is, no one can confirm your story," Suarez said. "Unless you can?" he asked, turning to me.

Luckily, Dave jumped in before I had to say anything. "Are you accusing me of something? Because if you are, you're wrong," he said.

"I'm simply trying to get some answers, including whether you knew this man," Suarez said, pointing to the photograph again.

Dave scowled. "We've been over this already," he said.

"Maybe this will jog your memory," Suarez said, pulling a credit card slip out of the folder. "It's a receipt for dinner at your restaurant last night."

I glanced inside the folder while Suarez wasn't looking. There was more stuff, including what looked like a rental car agreement, plus a sheet of stationery. I couldn't read the name on the stationery, but the logo was a picture of a covered wagon. Must have been another bill. Maybe from a hotel?

"What is your point, Detective?" Dave said. "So he ate

at Chez Isabelle. A lot of people eat at my restaurant. It doesn't mean anything."

"My point is, Mr. Keiller, that I think you did know him. His name was Aaron Sneider," said Suarez.

"Aaron Sneider?" said Dave.

It was a question, but more like a statement. Dave definitely knew this guy. My chest tightened another notch. *Aaron Sneider?* I tried to think, but the name didn't mean anything to me.

"Who . . . who was he?" I asked.

Suarez looked at me, surprised, like he'd forgotten I was there. "He was a journalist," he said. "Worked for a Boston-based scientific journal called *Particle*. He wrote this piece about fourteen years ago." Suarez pulled a photocopy from the folder. I tried to see what it said, but Dave blocked my view.

"Detective, I'm not sure where this is going, but could we . . . ?" he said, motioning toward me.

Suarez either didn't hear Dave or ignored him, because he kept talking. "I know it was a while ago, but it's not something you forget, is it, Mr. Keiller?"

"Remember what?" I said. "Dave, what's he talking about?"

"Okay, that's enough," said Dave. He pushed his chair

back. "Come on, Oz, we're going." He stood up. "Oz? Let's go," he repeated.

But I didn't move. The article was lying right in front of me on the table. I picked it up before anyone could stop me. I read the headline.

Traitor without a Cause
Leading U.S. Physicist Caught Stealing Nuclear Secrets

My heart beat faster as my eyes raced down the page. What was the big deal? Why didn't Dave want me to see it?

Under the headline was a photo of a man. Brown hair, brown eyes. Smiling like life was good. I recognized him, just like I'd recognized Dead Guy. Only this time the man in the photo was someone I knew. He was my father.

CHAPTER V

I stared at the article. I wasn't even reading it, just staring at the picture of my dad. Only *he* wasn't my dad. My dad was a good guy. Okay, so I never really knew him—I never even *met* him. He died before I was born. But I believed what everyone told me. It was a short list: He was a brilliant physicist at Los Alamos National Laboratory, and he'd died of a heart attack when Mom was pregnant with me.

It wasn't much, but it had been enough until now.

My head felt fuzzy, like I'd worked a killer shift at the restaurant. Slammed. Pummeled. Toast. Suddenly my dad was someone else. A liar, a thief . . . a traitor.

A buzz filled the air. It was Dave and Suarez over in a

corner of the room, arguing. Dave was jabbing his finger at Suarez. Suarez looked bored. Suddenly Dave turned and caught me watching him. The look on his face told me everything.

He knew.

He knew Dad was a spy but hadn't told me. My stomach twisted into a jumbo knot. And if Dave knew, then Mom knew. . . . I felt sick.

I thought about all the times I'd mentioned Dad's name, hoping Mom would tell me some story about him. I waited for her to tell me my grin was like his or that my voice reminded her of him. But she never did. She'd just look sad, like she was going to bawl, then Dave would glare at me like I'd done something wrong. So I stopped asking.

I was such an idiot. The problem was, they didn't want me to know the truth. It made me mental to think that Mom had lied to me all these years, but Dave . . . If what Mom did was bad, then what Dave did was ten times worse.

I mean, he was my *big brother*. He was supposed to look out for me, not lie through his teeth. The anger bubbled up inside me, and I couldn't stop it. Did he think I couldn't handle it? It was the story of my life—Dave trying to tell me what I could and couldn't do. But this . . . this was way too much.

Before I knew what I was doing, I stood up. My hand flew, scattering the papers.

I slammed my hand down on the table in rhythmic beats. "YOU. SHOULD. HAVE. TOLD. ME." I didn't even recognize my own voice.

Dave and Suarez turned quickly. Dave put out his hands to calm me, but it was too late. "Oz," he said. "I can explain everything. But not here. At home." He motioned toward the door.

My heart pounded against my rib cage like it was going to burst. Dave walked over to me. "Oz . . . please," he said, almost pleading. He placed his hand on my shoulder. I yanked it away.

"Don't touch me," I said.

Dave started to say something but didn't. Finally he shook his head and said, "I'll wait for you in the hall."

"Yeah, whatever," I muttered. I watched him walk away.

"Oz. . . ." It was Suarez. His voice broke through my brain fog.

"Yeah?" I said. I looked over at him.

He was leaning against the wall with his legs crossed.

He pushed himself off the wall and walked over until he was only a few feet from me.

"I'm sorry. I can see you're upset." His voice was slow, measured. "I know this is a lot to take in . . . the murder . . . your dad." He paused, waiting for me to say something. What did he want? Was he looking for a total breakdown? Tears? Well, he wouldn't get it. I clenched my jaw and forced myself to stare back.

"I've got a lot of respect for your brother. I do . . . I really do." He gave me a half smile, like Dave was the most amazing guy in the world. "Running the restaurant, keeping things going—it can't have been easy."

"Dave doesn't *run* the restaurant. He's the head chef. There's my mom and Razor and . . ." My voice trailed away. *Stop talking—you're whining, and you sound like a girl.*

Suarez waved his hands. "Sure, sure. I'm just saying that some hotshot journalist shows up in Santa Fe, years after he's written an article that destroys your family. So you ask yourself, What's this guy doing back here? Raking things up again? Looking for more dirt on your family? Maybe he's writing some new piece to bring back a lot of old ghosts."

Suarez shrugged. "Who knows," he said. "What I do

know is that he turns up at Chez Isabelle. That takes a lot of nerve after what he did. And if I'm your brother, I'm going to be upset—angry, even—because this guy could make things very difficult for me and my family. Rehash a lot of stuff from the past. He could destroy everything I'd—we'd—worked so hard to rebuild."

"So he ate at Chez Isabelle," I said. "That doesn't mean Dave knew him." I tried to sound convincing, but I didn't believe what I was saying—so why would Suarez?

"Didn't recognize the man who stitched up his own dad?" Suarez scowled and scrunched up his eyebrows. "Come on, Oz. You can do better than that."

"I don't know what you're talking about." I darted a glance down the hall. Now I wished I'd left with Dave. Why didn't he come back and do something? My hands were sweaty. I wiped them on my jeans, hoping Suarez wouldn't notice.

"Here's what I'm thinking. Aaron Sneider comes to the restaurant Friday night. He hangs out till closing. He waits until everyone has gone. Then he grabs your brother for a chat. Things get hot. Suddenly they're out of control. All that anger your brother felt for fourteen years boiled up and he couldn't control it. And you know what? Now he's in over his head. Things are bad, and he doesn't know how to make them right. But we can help him—you and me. Do you understand what I'm saying?" He paused but didn't take his eyes off me.

That's when it clicked. Suarez figured Dave had murdered Sneider. *And he thought I knew something.* My stomach lurched. I had to get out of there. "I gotta go," I stammered. "Dave's waiting for me."

"Sure, okay. Just remember Dave needs your help. And the best way you can help him is by telling us everything you know. *Everything.*"

"But I don't know anything," I blurted out, hoping he would believe me. But I did know something, didn't I? I had Sneider's note about the meeting with Dave. For a second I thought about spilling. It wasn't too late, was it? Tell Suarez the truth or make up some story about how I found the note. Let him deal with it. Besides, maybe he was right . . . maybe . . .

"Oz," Suarez said, interrupting my thoughts. "The longer this goes on, the worse it gets—for Dave, you, your mom, the restaurant. We handle this quickly, we minimize damage to your family and the business. If it drags on . . . well, that's when things get ugly. Suddenly no one wants to eat at your restaurant, and just like that"—he snapped his fingers—"it's all gone. It would be a shame to see that happen." For the second time that day, I thought I was going to spew.

Suarez pulled a card out of his breast pocket. "If you think of anything, call me—anytime." He handed me the card, then turned and walked back to the table. He gathered up his papers, ignoring me. I was invisible again.

I stared at the card like it was going to tell me what to do. I thought about what Suarez said. I thought about telling him the truth. I thought about what Dave had done . . . or hadn't done. I made my decision. I slipped the card into my backpack, next to the note I'd taken from Sneider's dead body. Then I walked out the door and didn't look back.

CHAPTER VI

"Why didn't you tell me?" I said.

I'd walked down the hall, even though I'd wanted to sprint to get away from Suarez. Dave was getting a drink from the water fountain near the main entrance of the police station. He stopped drinking and straightened up.

"You're upset," he said. "I get it. But I'm not up for this now." He started to turn away.

"Upset?" I grabbed his sleeve so hard he swung around, facing me. Dave was older than me, but I was almost as tall as he was. He looked at me like I'd slapped him. For a second, I wondered if I had.

"You and Mom lie to me my whole life and you think I'm *upset?* You don't get it, do you?" I said. My hands were trembling so badly that I had to clench my fists to stop them from shaking.

For a second we stared at each other. We've never been tight. We don't look alike. We don't think alike. Even when we're at the restaurant, we don't hang out. He's not like Razor, who you can talk to about anything. But he's always been my brother. Now he felt like a total stranger.

I let go of his arm.

"It's a long story." He frowned, like remembering gave him a headache. "I was twelve when you were born. It was the worst year of my life."

"Thanks," I muttered.

"That's not what I meant. I meant . . . the story came out . . . you know . . . about Dad. . . ." Dave's voice trailed off. He looked around to see if anyone was listening before he continued. "Dad's legal fees wiped out everything we had. Then he died. There was a small insurance policy, but that was it. Mom used it to open Chez Isabelle. Gran helped some. But it was hard."

"Still, you could have told me. I could have handled it."

Dave shook his head. "You don't know what it was like. Parents wouldn't let their kids play with me anymore. People avoided the restaurant. You could hear them whispering about us behind our backs. All we wanted was for it to go away. I didn't want you to go through what I did."

I heard what he said, but it wasn't good enough. Nothing was good enough anymore. "It still didn't give you the right to lie to me."

Dave squeezed his eyes shut. "I didn't lie. I—we—felt it was for the best. Mom would have told you eventually."

"Right, I forgot about Mom," I said sarcastically. "She knew—of course. But that's no surprise, since I figure the whole town knew. Everyone except yours truly. And you—and let's not forget Mom—decided I couldn't handle it. Thanks for nothing."

"Look, I'm sorry the way it came out. But you have no idea what you're talking about. None."

"Don't I? That's funny, because Detective Suarez thinks I do."

Dave's eyes flew open. I'd gotten his attention.

"Yeah, that's what we were talking about back there. He wants to know all about you, Dave. So maybe you're not as clever as you think you are."

"Don't talk to him," he snapped. "Do you understand? Don't talk to anyone. I'll handle this. Okay?"

"Great. Like you've handled things so far." I almost

mentioned the note, but I didn't. Not here, not with all these cops around. Besides, he'd probably just lie again. "So I guess you'll call Mom and tell her what's going on?" I was pushing him too far, but I didn't care.

His eyes flashed. "No one is telling Mom anything. Got it? Mom's got her hands full. I don't want you bugging her."

Now I felt like I was the one who'd been slapped. Was he serious? There was no way we could keep this from Mom. "But we've got to—"

Dave held his hand up to stop me talking and motioned toward the entrance to the station.

There were loud voices just outside the building.

"Come on," said Dave. "We can talk more at home." I nodded. A moment ago every muscle in my body was tensed—ready to fight. Suddenly I was so tired that all I wanted to do was crawl into bed and sleep for a month.

We walked outside. I squinted, trying to adjust to the bright sunshine. But it was more than just the sun. We were in the middle of a swirl of lights, microphones, and cameras. There were probably a dozen journalists and cameramen all around us. "You're joking," muttered Dave. I glanced over at him. We were thinking the same thing: Word was out about the murder at Chez Isabelle.

"Let's get out of here," Dave said. He jogged down the steps quickly, keeping his head down, ignoring the crowds.

I shot another glance at the pack of journalists. That's when I figured it out. They were swarming around someone, but it wasn't us. I heaved a sigh of relief. But now I was curious. What was the big deal? What was so interesting?

Dave waved at me impatiently from the bottom of the steps. *Hurry up*, his look said. I ignored him and edged closer to a cameraman so I could get a better view.

"CNN interview last week. Meeting with Santa Fe police this week. For someone who hasn't declared his candidacy, you sure look like you're running for office," one of the reporters called out.

I craned my neck to see who they were talking to. I knew him. It was Harrison Smith. He was hard to miss. Snow-white hair and jet-black eyebrows. A Chez Isabelle regular.

"Yeah, put us out of our misery. Are you a candidate for the U.S. Senate or not?" chimed in another reporter.

Harrison Smith twirled one of his cuff links and gave the journalist half a smile.

"Now, I told you folks, no comment. I'm here as

a private citizen today to meet with law enforcement officials. I share their concerns about the alarming rise in crime throughout New Mexico."

His voice boomed like he wanted to make sure no one missed a word. Smith was a hotshot business guy . . . something in defense, I think Mom said. He ate with a bunch of his buddies at Chez Isabelle once a month.

"Sounds like a campaign speech to me," called out another journalist. Some of the journalists laughed, and Smith smiled back. "If you do run, can we assume you'd back plans for boosting nuclear power production in New Mexico?"

"You know I've never made a secret about how important I think nuclear development is for the defense of our nation and to power our homes and businesses," said Harrison. "You hear a lot these days about renewable energy—wind, geothermal, and solar. Now, they're all fine, but their contribution to our total energy needs is tiny. We need to be practical, and that means nuclear. It's the only way forward." Then he smiled. "And you can quote me on that. I'm afraid that's all I've got time for. But I will be holding a press conference on Thursday. Come along then and I'll answer all your questions."

I snaked through a pool of reporters and headed down the steps. I glanced back one last time. Smith was still smiling, but this time he was ignoring the reporters. I blinked, then looked again to be sure I was right. I was. He was looking straight at me.

CHAPTER VII

I'd had enough of Dave, so I skipped the ride home. He looked relieved, like he was glad to ditch me, too. Instead I headed toward the plaza, the heart of downtown Santa Fe. I had an idea.

It felt good to be outside. The skies had cleared, and it was the kind of blue you only see out here. Now that it was September, town was less crowded. There were still some straggler tourists buying turquoise jewelry from the Native Americans sitting outside the Palace of the Governors. On the other side of the plaza, two caffeine-fueled soccer moms battled it out for a parking space while some Texans strolled into Packard's, ready to blow major cash on squash blossom belts.

I wove through the shoppers on San Francisco until I reached an entrance with a small wooden sign that read ARCHIBALD MCCALLISTER, ATTORNEY-AT-LAW. Archie is a big Chez Isabelle fan. In fact, he was there last night. He likes the food, but if you ask me, he likes my mom more. Or at least that's what Rusty says. I try not to think about it, but Archie's okay. I hoped I'd catch him in, even though it was Saturday.

I took the steps two at a time to his second-floor office. The waiting room was dark, but the door was unlocked so I walked in. His office ran along the front of the building overlooking the street. The lights were on, and he was sitting at his desk.

"Oz, come in, come in. You caught me having a late lunch." Archie tugged at a paper napkin tucked into his collar. He wiped his mouth and smiled. Archie had black hair that he wore swept back from his forehead and an over-the-top mustache that twirled up at the ends. He always wore a suit. Today it was a bow tie, suspenders, and a loud green-and-purple-striped shirt.

Definitely not subtle, but somehow he pulled it off. He caught me staring. "Savile Row. Got it last time I was in London," he said with his southern drawl. Archie was a transplant from New Orleans but hadn't lost his accent after five years in Santa Fe. He straightened his tie.

"Now to what do I owe this pleasure? Shouldn't you be playing a computer game or going to a rave or whatever it is y'all do these days?" He gave me a wink and a smirk.

"No raves today, Arch. I wasn't sure you'd be here, since it's a Saturday."

He jumped up and pulled over a chair. "Where are my manners? Sit, sit. I'm finishing up some paperwork for a case that comes to trial this week," he said.

He must have caught me eyeing his lunch, because he piped up, "Jambalaya made by yours truly. Please, help yourself."

I hadn't eaten anything and was starving. He slid a plate, fork, and knife over. I scooped out some shrimp and rice.

He waited until I'd finished eating before he said, "Now, why don't you tell me what's going on? Nothing's wrong, I hope? Your mother is all right, isn't she?"

"She's fine. Still with Gran. Mom found a convalescent home for her—you know, rehab and stuff for the stroke. It's in Alsace, where Gran's from, so she's happy about it."

"So then . . . ?" Archie said.

"It's something else." I wasn't sure what to say, so I

just jumped in. "Do you remember a guy at the restaurant last night? Maybe fifties . . . heavyset white guy, wearing chinos and a button-down . . . probably five-nine. Ate by himself . . . not a regular . . . out-of-towner."

"Vaguely. If he's the man I'm thinking of, we arrived at the same time. Late-ish . . . around eight thirty. He sat near the kitchen, which he seemed to like."

The main kitchen at Chez Isabelle is open to the dining room. Customers like to come and watch the action.

"Do you remember anything else about him?" I asked.

"Let's see. He had a bag with him . . . a laptop, I'd say." Archie stared off into space for a second, thinking. "I remember looking over at him one time and he was busy jotting something down in a notebook."

He gave his mustache a tug, smiled, and said, "If you ask me, he wasn't giving the food the proper attention it deserves. But what's with the twenty questions?" His face grew serious. "Nothing's wrong, is it?"

I hesitated, then blurted it out. "He's dead. Murdered. At Chez Isabelle. I—I found him. . . ." I told him the whole story . . . well, everything except the note. He didn't interrupt me, but he did grab a legal pad and write notes while I spoke.

When I finished, I said, "I thought you might have heard something . . . seen something . . . you know . . ."

Archie shook his head and sighed. "I'm afraid not. Oz, I can see what you're doing. You want to help, try to figure out what happened. But leave it to the police. Speaking of which, I don't want you or Dave speaking to them again without me there. Dave should have called me before answering any questions. And I'm going to track down your mom in France. She's got her cell phone, doesn't she?"

"Yeah, but Dave doesn't . . . ," I said.

"Doesn't what?"

"Doesn't want Mom to know."

He shook his head again. "Your brother thinks he can handle everything himself, doesn't he? Well, in this case, I have to disagree. He can't. And your mom needs to know."

Dave was going to kill me, but what could I do?

He glanced at his watch. "It's eight hours later in France. Too late to call your mom now, but I'll text her and call her first thing in the morning. I'll also give Detective Suarez a call and see what I can find out. Then we wait."

"But there's got to be something—"

He cut me off. "No, Oz. Leave it to the police. We

have to hope they get to the bottom of this before it gets any worse."

"Worse? You're kidding, aren't you?"

He shook his head. "I wish I were."

"How could it get any worse?"

"Where to begin? Civil lawsuits brought by the victim's family . . . wrongful death, that kind of thing. Not to mention the negative PR. I won't lie to you, Oz. It's a mess. And I don't like the way it looks. I'm sure the police don't either. I find it hard to believe that this man—Aaron Sneider—decides to eat at your restaurant, then winds up dead hours later. Why was he there?" he asked. "Now that's the real question."

CHAPTER VIII

I left Archie's office, trying to make sense of what he'd said. He was right. Why *was* Sneider at Chez Isabelle? He must have known we owned the restaurant. Just a coincidence he decided to eat there? No way.

I was so busy thinking about Sneider that it took me a second before I heard someone calling my name.

"Yo, Oz. Wait up, man." I spun around. It was Razor. He was dressed in regulation Razor: blue jeans, white T-shirt, and a serious pair of lizard-skin cowboy boots. Razor was . . . well, he was cool. There was something about him. Everyone wanted to hang with him. Even my mom liked him. She didn't even mind the goatee and silver earring.

He jogged up to me and clapped me on the shoulder. "I've been calling your name, but you were a million miles away."

"Yeah, I guess I was."

"Are you okay? I heard what happened."

"You heard?" I asked.

"Dave called, then the cops stopped by my place."

"The cops?"

"Yeah, they've been talking to all the staff. You know, getting statements."

"Tell me about it," I said. "I just spent the afternoon getting the third degree."

"So what's the deal? Do they know what happened?"

I gave Razor a quick recap. When I reached the part about my dad and Sneider's article, Razor's eyes got big. "It was *that* guy?"

"Dave didn't tell you when he called today?"

"No," said Razor.

"But you'd heard the story about my dad, hadn't you?"

"Yeah, sure I knew." He must have seen the look on my face. "You did know, didn't you?"

I chewed on my lip. "I just found out. Today. At the police station."

"Jeez, Oz. I thought you knew. I never mentioned it

because I figured you didn't want to talk about it."

"No, I was the last person on the planet to find out. Apparently Dave thought he was doing me a favor," I said.

Razor rubbed his chin and sighed. "He had no right, Oz. He should have told you."

I smiled. It was nice to have someone finally understand. No surprise that Razor would understand stuff that my own brother never did. But then my smile faded.

"It's just . . ."

"Just what? Oz, what's really bugging you?"

"How come I never figured it out . . . about my dad? It's not like Santa Fe is a big town or anything. People must have talked about what he did. How come I missed it?"

"Oz, it was a long time ago. Sure, people were all over it when it happened, but then there's another story in the news and they move on."

"But still . . ."

"Besides," Razor continued, "no one held what your dad did against you. Everyone admired your mom for starting Chez Isabelle. If anything, they felt sorry for her. The rest? It was ancient history." Razor shook his head. "And you need to forget about it too. Forget about Dave. And the cops? They've done their tough-guy routine. That's what they do. Hopefully they'll get their butts in gear now and find the guy who did this. Then we reopen Chez Isabelle, and everything is back to normal."

I hesitated. "I don't think it's going to be that simple."

Razor furrowed his brow. "I don't get it. What do you mean?"

I sighed. I thought I might as well tell him. "Dave's being all cagey about where he was last night."

"The cops don't think Dave—"

I interrupted him. "I'm not sure what they think."

Razor started to say something, then stopped.

"What? What is it?" I asked.

"Nothing. I was about to say, check with Carlos."

"You lost me."

"When I left last night, Dave and Carlos were holed up in his office."

"Dave and Carlos?" Carlos had been at Chez Isabelle for a couple of years. He did prep, dishes, cleanup—basically anything that needed to be done. But it wasn't like he and Dave were tight.

"I know. I thought it was weird too," Razor said. "But then Dave's been weird this whole week, hasn't he? And last night, did you see him? I thought he was going to go postal."

So he'd noticed too. I'd figured it was just the added pressure of Mom being away. With her gone, he was handling front of the house, waitstaff, reservations, that kind of thing—plus taking care of the kitchen. One job was too much, but both was out-of-control crazy.

"Maybe I'll give Carlos a call," I said.

"Don't bother. Dave asked me to call all the guys and tell them the restaurant was closed for a couple of days. I got everyone except Carlos."

"He should be around. He always does a Saturday shift."

"Yeah, I know, but I tried his home and cell." Razor shrugged again. "No luck. Where are you headed now?"

"Home. I just went to see Archie McCallister. He was at Chez Isabelle last night. Thought he might have seen something."

"Anything?" he asked.

"Not much." I told him what Archie had said. "You didn't see anything, did you? I mean, when you did the rounds of the tables last night?"

He cracked a smile. "A middle-aged white guy? No, but I did speak with a lovely young lady from Dallas."

I smiled back. "Right. Just thought you might have seen something."

There was one other thing. I thought about the note

I'd found on Sneider about the meeting with Dave. Maybe I should tell Razor.

He must have seen the look on my face. "You okay?" he asked.

I hesitated. Nothing fazed Razor. He never lost his cool. You could totally be in the weeds with orders piling up and he'd jump in and get the food out. Maybe he'd know what to do.

"Well, see, I—" Before I could say anything, his phone rang. He looked at the number on the screen and then back at me.

"I gotta take this one. Catch you later?"

"Yeah, later," I said.

I gave him a wave and started down San Francisco. I thought again about the note. I looked back one last time before turning onto Galisteo, but he was still on the phone.

No biggie. I could always tell him later. But for now, the note would stay my secret.

CHAPTER IX

I wasn't looking forward to seeing Dave back at home. He'd lied to me about Dad, and I was pretty sure he was lying about last night. There was something he wasn't telling me and the police, but I didn't know what.

I was in luck. The house was quiet, and there was no sign of him. I kept playing over what had happened, hoping it would make sense. But it didn't. My brain was fried and I couldn't focus.

It was like when Dave and Razor got slammed on a busy Saturday night. By the time the last guest left, they'd be totally obliterated. Only problem was, it was tough to wind down. So Dave stayed late planning menus and doing paperwork. Razor, on the other hand, went to El Farol to hang out and listen to some local bands.

I had my own way of dealing. I changed into running shorts and an old T-shirt. I did some quick stretches, locked the house, and jogged up Garcia. I started slowly, then picked up the pace when I hit Camino del Monte Sol and Santa Fe Prep. By the time I reached the St. John's College parking lot I'd hit my stride. I picked up the trail and darted between the junipers and clumps of chamisa in full blossom. An old guy was walking his two dogs in the arroyo, but aside from him, I had the place to myself.

About a mile in, the trail went vertical. Mount Atalaya shoots up almost two thousand feet. Hiking isn't too bad—a couple of hours round trip. But running—or sprinting—makes your lungs burn and kills your legs.

Just what I needed.

When I reached the top I could barely breathe, and my shirt was soaked. It was close to six p.m., and the sun was starting to sink. Rain clouds were over the Jemez Mountains and probably heading our way. I touched my lucky rock like I always did, then I slumped down on the ground to catch my breath before the downhill run.

All day I'd been thinking about my dad. I tried not to, but I couldn't help it. This whole mess—Sneider's murder,

Dave and whatever he'd done—was his fault, wasn't it? He'd messed up, and now we were paying the price. And what for? I was angry, and angry at someone I'd never met and never would meet.

I gazed out at the mountains and forced myself to take in a couple of deep breaths. I'd have to figure out all this stuff about my dad. I knew that. But not now. Now I needed to figure out what happened at Chez Isabelle last night.

I got back up and headed down the mountain. My head was clearer. I made a mental list of what I knew and didn't know. The second list was a lot longer.

Aaron Sneider—some science journalist from Boston—eats at our restaurant on Friday night. In his pocket, he's got a note about a meeting with Dave at midnight. Sometime early Saturday morning, he's murdered. But why was he meeting Dave? And why so late? And what was the deal with Carlos and Dave?

I had a creepy thought. If Dave and Sneider *had* met, then Dave was one of the last people to see Sneider alive. I bet Suarez would say Dave was the last one, wouldn't he?

That was the problem. The note didn't look good. Dave was a jerk and a pain, but a murderer? *Admit it,* I thought. *Dave had a serious temper.* He'd fly off the handle if the produce order was late. So what would he have done when Sneider showed up at Chez Isabelle?

I hit a sharp turn too quickly and skidded on some loose stones. I got my balance back and kept going, picking up speed on a flat stretch of trail.

I thought about this journalist, Aaron Sneider. He wrote a piece about Dad and then, thirteen years later, he decides to come to Santa Fe for a visit? Just happens to have dinner at our restaurant? Archie was right. It didn't make any sense. It was too much of a coincidence.

I rounded the last bend and saw the St. John's campus. It was getting dark, and the parking lot was empty. I slowed down to a jog. My muscles burned but my head felt better.

Maybe the police would figure out what happened, maybe not. I was sure that Suarez had decided Dave was guilty. If he found out about the note, he'd be 100 percent sure. Another nail in Dave's coffin. But why wasn't Suarez trying to figure out who this guy was and what he was doing here?

If they weren't going to, then I was. A small voice in my head whispered, *But what if Dave was involved? What if the police are right? What then?*

I didn't know. I might find out something I didn't want to. It was a chance I had to take.

CHAPTER X

After my run, I scrounged around the kitchen until I found a can of soup. Rusty thought it was weird we never had any food at home, but why bother? We always ate at Chez Isabelle, because it was more home than home. I balanced the bowl of soup on my lap while I Googled my dad. There were a bazillion results, but after the first couple of pages I got the drift. Funny thing was, I'd never done this before. I could have found out the truth whenever I wanted, but I guess I never looked because I didn't know there was anything to look for.

I printed out a couple of pages and stuck them in a plastic folder. I grabbed an old copy of the Yellow Pages and leafed through it until I found what I was looking for. I ripped it out, added it to the folder, and put the folder in my backpack. I left another message for Rusty around eleven, then headed to bed.

The phone rang just as I was about to turn out the lights.

"Hello?"

"Oz, it's Mom."

"Mom? Did you hear what happened?"

"I just got off the phone with Archie, and he told me everything. Are you all right? You're not hurt, are you?"

"I'm fine. I mean, it's bad, but I'm okay. Mom, when are you coming home?"

"I wish I were there right now, love. The problem is that Gran had another stroke. It was a small one, but the doctors want me to stay with her until she's stabilized."

"So what does that mean?"

"A few more days at the most. I'll get there as soon as I can, I promise. Is Dave still up?"

"Dave? He's not here."

"*What?* You're alone? Dave left you by yourself? I'll call Archie and have him come over."

Her voice was in total panic mode. I jumped in quickly.

"Mom, no. I don't need a babysitter."

"Oz, someone murdered a man in our restaurant and you found the body. I don't want you by yourself until they track down whoever did this."

Murdered a man? Mom said it like Sneider was a complete stranger, like she didn't know who he was. Suddenly the relief I'd felt when I first heard her voice faded. Instead I felt anger at her for all the lies she'd told me.

"The dead guy has a name, Mom. It's Aaron Sneider. You know who he is, don't you?"

There was a slight pause before she spoke. "Yes . . . I know who he is. Oz, I'm sorry. I'm sorry you had to find out this way."

"Me too. Not every day you find out your dad is a traitor."

"I was going to tell you when the time was right."

"*When the time was right?* Guess it's too late for that now."

"Oz, I know you're angry and you have every right to be. And you probably have a lot of questions for me. I promise I'll answer them all, but not right now. Right now, I need your help. I need you and Dave to work together to keep Chez Isabelle going."

"Chez Isabelle? What do you mean?"

"Oz, everything we have is in the restaurant, every penny we own. Something like this could kill the restaurant. And if we lose Chez Isabelle, we lose everything."

Suddenly everything that Suarez and Archie had said came crashing in around me. As bad as things were, they could get worse—we could lose Chez Isabelle.

"Oz, are you there?"

"Yeah, I'm here."

"I'm sorry to be so blunt, but you need to understand how serious things are. I need your help to keep things going, so I'm asking you to put aside how you feel about me, your dad, all of this, until later. I know it's a lot to ask, but I have to know I can count on you. So can I? Can I trust you?"

"Yes," I said. "You can trust me." I knew that no matter what I felt and what she'd done, it was a promise I meant to keep.

SUNDAY

CHAPTER XI

I dragged myself out of bed early Sunday morning. I told myself to forget about Mom, Dave, Dad, all of it. *Focus on the plan.* I threw on some clothes, grabbed my backpack, and slipped past Dave's door. He must have gotten home after I'd gone to bed last night.

I rode down Garcia to Downtown Sub and ordered OJ and a muffin. It was the early crowd—a mixed bag of runners and senior citizens getting their lattes and *New York Times.* The only sound was the barista releasing steam into a jug of milk. No Rusty, so I headed for the patio.

I found her lounging around like she owned the place. She was leaning back in a white plastic chair with her legs stretched out on a small table in front of her.

She had on lime green combat boots and some floral top that clashed with her long carrot-colored hair. A pair of enormous black sunglasses covered her face.

"Where's the fire?" she asked. The sunglasses slipped down her nose, revealing green eyes.

"Sorry. I know it's early."

"*Verrrrry* early, so it better be good." She reached over and grabbed the muffin off my plate and took a bite.

"Help yourself," I said. "Where were you yesterday? I tried you all day. Didn't you get my text?"

"Sorry about that," said Rusty, talking with her mouth full. "My parents made me go up to Los Alamos for a no-nukes protest. They chained themselves to a fence— can you believe it? I was so embarrassed. And then the battery on my phone died. Basically, a lousy day."

"My lousy day beats yours."

She raised an eyebrow. "Spill," she said. She dabbed at a bunch of crumbs on her shirt. I unzipped my backpack, pulled out the note I'd found in Sneider's pocket, and handed it to her.

She read it, then looked up at me. "And?"

"*And* I found this in a man's pocket *and* the man was dead *and* he was in our walk-in fridge."

Rusty yanked her feet off the table and sat up straight,

shifting her shades to headband mode. I'd gotten her attention.

"And . . . ?" she asked.

"And I need your help to find out who killed him."

I told her the whole story. She grabbed a black Moleskine notebook out of her backpack. While I talked, she scribbled notes. Every now and then she'd pause and twirl a strand of hair absentmindedly. She was totally into it. Rusty was a forensics junkie—*CSI* (New York, Miami, Vegas), books, magazines—the works. So maybe my life was down the toilet, but at least I was making Rusty happy.

When I finished, I gulped down some OJ and looked over at her. She ran her finger around the plate and picked up the last muffin crumbs, then leaned back.

"I thought my parents were weird, but they're nothing. Your dad was a *spy*. . . ." She flicked back a strand of hair, narrowed her eyes and nodded her head in appreciation. "That totally rocks."

Great. Now Rusty thought my criminal dad was cool. "What I don't get is, what is there to steal at Los Alamos?" I asked. "Do you walk out with a nuclear warhead, some paper clips, and a legal pad?"

Rusty's eyes went enormous, like huge plates.

"You're amazing," she said. "Do you listen to *anything* in class?"

"Do I have to answer that?" I asked.

Rusty ignored me and continued, "Okay, so here's the deal. Los Alamos National Laboratory opened in the early forties. It was part of this über-top-secret program called the Manhattan Project. The U.S. and Germany were in this crazy race in World War II to see who could build the first nuclear bomb."

"But we didn't drop the bomb on Germany."

"Yeah, but get this. Germany surrendered, but we were still at war with Japan."

"So we dropped it on Japan."

"Actually, we dropped two bombs. The first bomb was called Little Boy. It was dropped on Hiroshima in early August 1945. Three days later, Fat Man was dropped on Nagasaki. The bombs killed thousands of people, and loads more died from radiation sickness afterward."

"Thanks for the history lesson," I said. "But that was way before my dad worked there. He didn't start at Los Alamos until the eighties."

"World War II ended, but Los Alamos didn't. There was a massive nuclear arms race with the USSR during the Cold War. Los Alamos was at the heart of it."

"But that's over too, isn't it?"

Rusty nodded. "I think my dad said the last U.S. nuclear bomb test was in the early nineties. But the U.S. still has a nuclear arsenal, and Los Alamos still does weapons research."

"But what's so hush-hush? What could my dad steal that was so important?"

"Oz, the place is filled with classified documents— like how to make a bomb. It's all super hush-hush. That's why Los Alamos is called the Secret City. No one really knows half the stuff that goes on up there."

I always pictured my dad as a nerdy scientist. But now he was a thief, a traitor. There was that sick feeling in the pit of my stomach. I wished I'd never heard of Sneider or Los Alamos or any of it.

"So the note?" Rusty asked, breaking through my thoughts. "You took it off the dead guy."

"I had to," I said.

"Then you lied to the police."

"I didn't lie. They didn't ask."

Rusty rolled her eyes. "You know you've totally broken about a million laws, don't you?" she said.

I swallowed. "I didn't have a choice."

"You sound like a politician." She paused, then said,

"You think he did it?" I didn't have to ask who "he" was.

"No. Dave didn't. He couldn't," I answered. I tried to sound convincing but wasn't sure I pulled it off.

"Did you tell anyone else what happened?"

"I was going to call Zach." He was a good friend of mine from school. "But I didn't want anyone else to know. Not now . . . not yet."

She looked at me for a second, then nodded. "Good idea. He'd tell the whole school." She pulled the page I'd ripped out of the phone book from my plastic folder. "Silver Dollar Motel," she said, tracing her fingers over the logo of the covered wagon in the ad. "This where we're going?" I nodded again. She leaned over and picked up her backpack and gave it a pat. "Lucky I brought my kit with me."

"Kit?"

"Never mind . . . just a couple of things for our life of crime."

I swallowed hard again. Okay, so it was a joke, but maybe this wasn't such a great idea. Rusty strode off to the parking lot and hopped on her bike. I eased myself out of my chair and followed her. I hoped my plan would work. If not, I was about to get me—and her—into a lot of trouble.

CHAPTER XII

The sign at the entrance read SILVER DOLLAR MOTEL. WHERE YOU'RE ALWAYS AT HOME. DAY AND WEEKLY RATES. I slowed down, pointed to the right, and we shot into the parking lot.

"Now what?" Rusty asked.

"We have to figure out which room was Sneider's," I said. The Silver Dollar's rooms were arranged in a U shape on two levels around a central parking lot. Each room opened onto a covered walkway. Hanging baskets full of flowers decorated the iron railings that ran the length of the walkways.

To the left of us was the office. Next to it was a minute kidney-shaped swimming pool and slide. "Won't someone see us?" Rusty said, pointing toward the office. The front of the office was completely glass. From inside you'd have a perfect view of the parking lot and all the rooms.

"You know Tommy Mariani?"

"Yeah. Neanderthal junior? Couldn't even pass art class," said Rusty.

"Yep, that one. You're looking at his favorite place to skateboard."

"You lost me," said Rusty.

"He says an old couple owns the place. The husband is practically deaf and does the night shift. Only he likes to take a nap in the back. So Mariani figures it's the perfect place for a late-night skateboarding session. If a guest tries to complain, it takes them forever to wake up the old guy. By the time they do, Mariani's gone." I glanced at my watch. "He should be on duty until eight o'clock, which gives us an hour to get in and get out."

We hid our bikes behind a Dumpster near the entrance. It wasn't hard to figure out which room was Sneider's. I spied the bright yellow police tape in the far right-hand corner. No one was guarding the door, and no cop cars were in the parking lot. I hoped they'd cleared out. I kept scanning the rooms, but everything was quiet—it looked like we were the only ones awake.

The police tape ran from the door to a column on the edge of the walkway, then back to the room. We climbed underneath it. I turned and checked out the other side of the motel again. No one watching. I reached for the doorknob, but Rusty grabbed my arm and shook her head. She set her backpack on the ground, unzipped it, and pulled out two pairs of plastic surgeon's gloves.

"You're kidding," I whispered.

"You want your fingerprints all over a crime scene, genius?" she said as she pulled hers on.

"Whatever," I said, tugging on a pair.

I was about to try the door again when I heard a noise. I leaned out and saw a housekeeper pushing a cleaning cart along the upstairs walkway. I jerked my head back. She hummed softly to herself, paused, then kept walking. I was pretty sure she hadn't seen me. I turned back to the door.

My heart pounded. Now that we were here, I was having second thoughts. If we were caught, we were in big trouble. But I didn't have a choice. I placed my hand on the doorknob and turned. It didn't budge—locked. I'd never even thought about the door being locked.

Rusty shrugged her shoulders. "Plan B?"

There was a window to the left of the door. I tried, but it was locked too. Maybe there was a way in around back? I looked at my watch—seven fifteen. We didn't have much time. Then I had an idea.

"Stay here." I slipped back under the police tape. I scanned the rooms again. A curtain fluttered in a room across the parking lot. I squinted but couldn't see anyone. I hoped it was the AC and not someone watching us.

I cruised down the walkway and up two flights of stairs to the second floor. The housekeeping cart was all the way at the end—almost directly over Sneider's room. I jogged toward it, trying not to make any noise. As I got closer, I heard the maid singing from inside the room.

My eyes raced over the cart. Toilet paper, mini soaps wrapped in plastic, a stack of *What's On Santa Fe* guides . . . there it was . . . on top of a pile of clean towels . . . a flat plastic passkey. I hoped it worked for all the rooms. I snapped it up, then leaned over the railing.

"Psst. Rusty." She looked up. I waved the key and she smiled. She ducked under the tape. I let the key card drop. She caught it. But then something happened. The humming stopped. Had the maid heard me? I froze. Frantically I looked for someplace to hide. I was trapped. If I ran back down the corridor, the maid would see me. The cart blocked the only other way out.

Seconds passed. Drops of sweat ran down my face. I

held my breath. Nothing. Then the humming started again. Water ran in the bathroom. A toilet flushed. I took a deep breath and leaned back over the railing. The door was open—Rusty was in. There wasn't much time. The maid would finish cleaning the room any minute now. I had to get the key back on the cart before she realized it was missing. I ran downstairs, taking the stairs two, three at a time.

I didn't bother to make sure the coast was clear. I didn't have time. I sprinted to the room. Rusty was inside. She'd pulled her hair back and was wearing an NYPD baseball cap she'd bought on the Internet. "Quick," I whispered. "The key."

She looked confused until I pointed upstairs. She nodded and tossed me the key.

Back up the stairs. Down the walkway. Almost there. The humming was louder, closer, coming toward me. It was too late. I wasn't going to make it. The maid had finished cleaning the room. No way I'd get to the cart before she did. I tore off the plastic gloves and shoved them in my pocket.

Just then the maid walked out of the room and saw me. Busted. She gasped and crossed herself.

"Uh, sorry. Didn't mean to scare you," I panted. I tried to catch my breath. She looked scared, like I was some kind of psycho. She had on a pale gray uniform, and her black hair was pulled back in a tight bun. Probably Dave's age, maybe younger. I smiled and tried to look normal. "My parents want some ice." I pointed to the stack of blue plastic ice buckets.

She smiled cautiously and nodded. Congratulations. I'd been downgraded from serial killer to nut job. Before she could hand me one, I said, "I got it." I grabbed one but managed to knock over the whole stack.

"Sorry . . . sorry . . . I'm a real klutz." I bent down and picked up the buckets and placed them back on the trolley along with the passkey. "Sorry about that." She gave me the pity smile. Now I wasn't even a nut job—just some pathetic loser with no coordination. I smiled back, said thanks, and started to walk away.

"Excuse me, *señor*." I froze. She knew I'd taken the key. Or she'd spotted the gloves. Why did I ever take them in the first place? I took a deep breath and slowly turned around. How was I going to get out of this? She eyed me curiously.

"Yes . . . ?" I answered.

"The ice machine . . . it's over there," she said, pointing to an alcove behind her.

I breathed again. "Thanks. Totally forgot." I smiled again and headed the right way.

CHAPTER XIII

Sneider's motel room was dark. There was a narrow strip of light where the curtains didn't meet, but that was it. I hit the light button on my Ironman watch—7:40. Only twenty minutes before the day manager came on duty.

"Catch," said Rusty, tossing me a flashlight. I flicked it on and did a quick tour of the room. Pretty basic: bed, bedside table, TV, chest of drawers, closet, and bathroom. Not exactly expense account material.

"Find anything?" I asked.

"No, not yet," she said. "I checked out the bathroom, but it looks like the police took everything. Clothes are gone too. See if you can find anything on your side of the room."

I squatted and panned the flashlight along the floor. The air-conditioning was off, so the room was hot and stuffy. I wiped my forehead on my sleeve and knelt down by the bed. The police—I guessed—had pulled the bedspread and sheets off so all that was left was a gray striped mattress. It was clean under the bed except for a couple of jumbo dust balls.

My heart sank. I was an idiot. We weren't going to find anything, because there wasn't anything to find. The police had taken anything important with them. Besides, we were running out of time. We had to get out of there. I yanked open the drawer to the bedside table. It was empty except for a dog-eared Gideon Bible.

I picked up the Bible and flipped through it—nothing. I tried to put it back in the drawer but it stuck. I tried again. No go. I was about to shove it in when I figured out what the problem was. Something was blocking the way. I crouched down and shone the flashlight inside the drawer. There it was: a business-size envelope taped to the top of the drawer. I must have caught the corner with the Bible.

"Rusty . . . over here."

She bent down beside me and flashed her light next to mine. Without saying a word, she reached over and teased the envelope away without tearing the tape. I reached for it, but she pulled it away. "Not so fast." She slipped it into a large plastic bag and sealed it.

"Come on, let me look," I said.

"Not until I fingerprint it."

"You are joking, aren't you?"

She was about to say something when we heard voices outside. "Kill the lights," I whispered. We switched them off. I put my flashlight on the bedside table and edged over to the window. Through the slit I made out three—no, four people. They were packing up their SUV, probably checking out. Car doors slammed and they drove off. I motioned to Rusty. "We gotta get out of here." She nodded. She slid over to the door and opened it slowly. I scanned the parking lot, then nodded. Rusty left, then me. I checked to make sure the door locked behind us.

It wasn't until we'd slipped under the police tape that I saw an old guy walk out of the office and into the parking lot. It must have been the owner of the motel. I looked at my watch. 7:55. Great. He should have been sleeping.

"Keep walking," I said. A row of cars parked on our side gave us some cover but not enough. If he looked this way, he'd see us.

"Down," I whispered. Rusty and I ducked and scurried along the walkway. "We gotta move fast." We hit the end of the walkway and ran the last few yards to the Dumpster. My heart raced. "You got the envelope?" I panted.

Rusty nodded, trying to catch her breath. "Safe and sound." She unzipped her backpack and reached a hand toward me. "Give me your flashlight," she said.

"Flashlight?" My heart sank. "I thought you had it. . . ." I'd forgotten the flashlight. It was on the bedside table in Sneider's room. I looked back toward the room.

Rusty shook her head. "No way. Just leave it, okay?" I looked at her. She was right, but still . . . We got on our bikes and off-roaded it to avoid the entrance. I almost turned around to look back but didn't.

My hands were sweaty on the handlebars. *There's nothing you can do about it*, I told myself. But I'd screwed up big-time. What if someone found the flashlight? No way to know. I'd have to wait and see. And what was in the envelope? Whatever it was, I hoped it was worth it.

CHAPTER XIV

"You were up early," said Dave.

"And you were home late," I shot back. I tossed my backpack on a kitchen stool and walked over to the fridge. Rusty and I had split up when we left the motel. We agreed to meet up at her place later.

I opened the fridge door expecting zippo, but it was full. Okay, not full, but not empty. Dave must have gone to the supermarket. I grabbed a carton of milk and unscrewed the top. "Glass, please," said Dave, without looking up from what he was doing. Papers were spread all over the counter. I filled a glass and gulped down half of it.

Dave picked up the phone and dialed.

"Could I speak with Mr. Wilson, please? ... Mr. Wilson,

it's David Keiller from Chez Isabelle. I'm calling because unfortunately, we won't be opening this evening. . . . Yes, I know it's last minute. I'm very sorry."

I set the glass down. The milk soured in my mouth. There was a full page of names and numbers in front of Dave, reservations for lunch and dinner that had to be canceled.

" . . . the police investigation? No, nothing to do with us. Mr. Wilson, I do have space next weekend. Would you like me to rebook you? . . . I understand, yes, of course. Well, we hope to see you soon, and again, apologies."

Dave hung up the phone. Neither one of us said anything. What was there to say? Dave crossed out the name. He looked like hell. He'd showered and shaved but just like he was going through the motions. He had dark circles under his eyes. He took a swig of coffee and cleared his throat.

"How bad is it?" I asked.

He looked over at me and sighed. "We had to cancel Saturday lunch and Saturday dinner—our biggest night. Now I'm canceling all the reservations for today. I just spoke to the police. They said they won't finish up until tomorrow at the earliest, so that's two more meals shot."

"Can't we do something?" I asked.

Dave frowned. "Not unless you've got another

restaurant kicking around. Then I've got to call the suppliers and try to cancel tomorrow's delivery. Probably too late, so that's more money down the drain." He scratched at the bandage on his hand.

I wanted to ask Dave about his hand but didn't. I could tell he wasn't in the mood. Besides, I had something more important to ask him about: the note. I had to find out why he was meeting Sneider.

"Dave . . . I need to tell you something . . . about the murder. . . ."

Dave interrupted. "It's okay. I know. I know what you did," he said.

Every muscle in my body tensed. He knew?

"But—but how . . . ? I don't get it."

"Archie called me. Told me all about your visit."

I squeezed my eyes shut tight. "Dave . . . it's not that—"

He interrupted me. "I won't lie. I wasn't happy. I was really ticked off that you went to see him behind my back."

"I didn't go behind your back," I blurted out. "I just thought he might have seen something, since he was there Friday night."

Dave shook his head. "It doesn't matter. I went by his office yesterday evening and we talked. And . . . well, you were right." *I was right?* "And I spoke to Mom this morning," he continued before I could say anything. "She said she spoke to you last night."

Before I could answer, the doorbell rang. I went to the front door and opened it. It was Razor.

"Hey, man, sorry I had to take that call yesterday," he said. "You doing okay?" He had on blue jeans and an old Grateful Dead T-shirt. His black hair was slicked back like he'd just gotten out of the shower.

"No worries," I said. "You here to see Dave?"

"Yeah, is he around?"

"In the kitchen. But warning: He's not in a great mood."

He leaned toward me and lowered his voice. "News flash. Your brother's always in a bad mood." He smiled and winked.

"Razor. Thanks for coming over," Dave said when we walked back into the kitchen. "And thanks for getting ahold of the guys yesterday. I appreciate it."

I stared at Dave and Razor for a second. Sometimes it's hard to believe they've been friends since high school. First, that Dave has any friends is incredible since he's so uptight. But also, you can't get more radical than Razor. After high school, Dave did the traditional thing. Went to the CIA— Culinary Institute of America—and did internships at uptight French restaurants. Razor? He headed to San

Francisco and worked in Napa. Then he traveled through Asia and South America and ate some weird, weird stuff.

The things he'd done would blow your mind. He'd cooked during a hurricane with no electricity ("Practically had to cook the food with a Bic lighter," he said.). He ended up in DC, then moved back to Santa Fe about a year ago. He'd been at Chez Isabelle ever since.

"Everyone's cool," Razor said. "A couple of the guys got visits from the cops, which freaked them out, but they're okay. Still no luck getting Carlos. Any idea how I can get ahold of him?"

"I gave him a few days off," said Dave. His voice was suddenly cold and sharp.

"You did?" asked Razor. "Only he was down for a double shift Saturday and Sunday, so I figured—"

Dave cut in. "Don't worry about Carlos, okay?" He turned around and poured two cups of coffee. Razor shot me a look as if to say, *See what I mean?*

Dave handed Razor a cup. Razor dumped a couple of spoonfuls of sugar in and stirred it. He kept talking, trying to fill in the dead air.

"Cops stopped by my place late yesterday," he said. "Kept going on about when everybody arrives at work, who gets there first, that kind of thing."

Dave looked up. His face was hard. "What did you tell them?"

Razor paused, weighing up what he was saying. "I told them Oz does a clean some Saturdays, then a prep cook arrives, and you're in around nine o'clock. They were all jazzed up about why you showed up so early yesterday. I said you could show up whenever you wanted—it's your restaurant, right?"

Dave started stacking the papers on the counter neatly. He didn't look up. "I appreciate your help, but in the future, direct any questions to me. That goes for all the staff."

Razor's face went red and his jaw tightened. Dave could be such a jerk. Razor was only trying to help.

Razor shook his head slightly and set his coffee cup down. "Sure, no problem. Dave, you know I'd do anything for Chez." He looked at his watch and said, "Look, I better go. Thanks for the coffee. I'll check in tomorrow to see how things are going, okay?"

Dave looked up. "Looks like Tuesday to reopen, but I'll confirm as soon as I know."

Razor nodded and headed back down the hall. I followed him. At the door he turned to say good-bye. "Look . . . about Dave," I said. I fumbled around trying to think of something to say. "It's just . . . he's under a lot of pressure and—"

Razor stopped me. "Hey, no sweat—really. Dave and I go way back. It's cool, I promise. Just remember, it's not your problem. It's Dave's. Okay?"

I nodded my head. "Thanks."

"No worries." Razor said. He smiled, turned, and left. I leaned against the door for a minute before I went back to the kitchen.

I'd barely stepped into the kitchen when the doorbell rang again. I cruised back down the hall and swung the door open, figuring that Razor had forgotten something. But it wasn't Razor. It was Detective Suarez. I felt like slamming the door shut.

"I have a warrant for the arrest of David Keiller Jr.," he said. I stood there, unable to say anything. *This isn't happening.* But when I looked at Suarez, I knew it was. His face was stony—no smiles, no nothing.

"What are you talking about?" I turned around. It was Dave. He was standing next to me.

Suarez looked straight at Dave. "We found the murder weapon—in a trash can near Chez Isabelle," said Suarez. My chest was heavy and it was hard to breathe, like I'd had the wind knocked out of me.

"And . . . ?" Dave said. He acted like everything was cool, but I could hear his voice catch slightly. Inside, my stomach was doing flips.

"Recognize it?" said Suarez. He showed Dave a photograph. Long blade. Carbon steel. Rosewood handle. I recognized it. . . .

"It's mine. What about it?" Dave said. Gran had given it to Dave when he graduated from the CIA.

Suarez's eyes narrowed. "You admit it?"

Dave's face didn't show anything, but I could tell he was rattled. "It doesn't mean anything. Anyone could—"

Suarez stopped him. "Before you say anything else, you might want to speak to a lawyer, Mr. Keiller."

Dave looked at me for a second. He tried to look calm, but we both knew this was serious. "Call Archie." That's all he said.

They snapped handcuffs on Dave and read him his rights. As they were leading him out, Suarez looked at Dave and said, "Just so you know, Mr. Keiller, we found only one set of prints on the knife—yours."

Dave didn't say anything and neither did I. I watched the squad car pull out of the driveway, turn, and drive off. Dave was gone. And for the first time in my life, I was completely alone.

CHAPTER XV

Rusty always asked me why I wanted to be a chef. The hours are horrible, the pay is lousy, and the pressure is intense. And she was right. It's hard to explain, but at the restaurant everything was clear, everything made sense. The order was ready or you were in the weeds. A sauce was seasoned perfectly or not. The customer loved you or hated you.

It was black and white and I liked that. You couldn't hide in a kitchen. Now all I wanted to do was hide. Nothing was clear and nothing made sense. Dave had been arrested. Cops had scoured our home for evidence linking him to Sneider's murder. They even talked about calling in social services. Luckily, Archie had shown up.

They agreed that I could stay with Rusty and her family until Mom got home.

The only good thing was that the police hadn't checked my backpack. If they had, they would have found Sneider's note. I had the note, and Rusty had the envelope I'd found in Sneider's motel room. That was it. That was all we had to go on. After everyone left I sat in the kitchen, staring at the wall. Finally I got up, washed out the coffee cups, and wiped the counters.

My cell rang. "You coming over?" It was Rusty. Her voice was soft, almost a whisper.

"Sorry, I should have left already. I'll take off now."

"No worries, whenever . . . Mom's glad you're coming to stay. . . . You okay with the couch?"

"Sure . . . the couch is good."

"When you get here, we can take a look at the envelope, see what's inside." Rusty tried to sound excited. It was hard, but I tried to sound excited too.

"That's great, definitely."

"Oz . . . there's something else. . . ."

"Yeah . . . ?"

"Just to warn you . . . it's tofu casserole for dinner." I could feel her smiling on the other end of the line.

I smiled too. "I'll pick something up to eat," I said. I grabbed some clothes from my room, stuffed them in my backpack, and walked to the front door. I turned and took one last look at my home, then left, locking the door behind me.

CHAPTER XVI

I got to Rusty's by four. Before I even closed the gate, her mom was there. She didn't say anything, just cupped my face in her hands and stared into my eyes. Her hands were warm and rough and smelled like lavender. I used to get embarrassed when she did this. Rusty said it was something about passing positive energy from her to me. Weird? Yeah, okay. But after everything that had happened, I figured I could use all the positive energy I could get.

She let go and grabbed my hand. "Come. I want to give you something." One of the cats—looked like Portia—leaped out from a rosemary plant as we walked up the stone path to the house. Dozens of wind chimes clanged in the breeze, and broken bits of mirror and old CDs hung from the fruit trees to scare away birds. Inside, it took a second for my eyes to adjust to the darkness.

"Here," she said, pressing something into my hands. It was a dried bundle of twigs.

"Uh . . . thanks . . . ," I stammered. "It's . . ." I wanted to say, *It's dead,* but didn't.

She smiled. "It's a sage smudge stick. Light it inside Chez Isabelle to purify it from all negativity."

I wasn't sure what to say.

"She means all the blood sprayed everywhere," said Rusty, leaning over the split-rail banister.

"Thanks. I kinda figured," I said. I tucked it in my backpack and headed upstairs.

"Don't forget—dinner in an hour," her mom sang up after us.

"Food. Please. Now," Rusty said. She was swiveling around in her desk chair like she was on a fairground ride.

"Chill, okay? What do you eat when I'm not around to be your personal delivery service, anyway?" I swung my backpack onto her bed and unzipped it. I pulled out a plastic container and a spoon and dropped it on the desk. "Chocolate mousse," I said. I reached into my backpack and whipped out a can. "And Diet Coke. As ordered." I tossed her the can.

She caught the DC, popped it open, and took a gulp. She flicked the lid off the mousse, ran her finger across the top, then licked it clean.

"Aren't you eating?" she asked.

"Not hungry," I said. My stomach was queasy. And watching Rusty attack the mousse was almost more than I could handle.

She stopped mid-mouthful and stared at me.

It freaked me out when she did this, staring at me like I was an animal at the zoo. "What? What's your problem?" I said.

She set the mousse down on her desk. "Want to talk about it?" she asked.

I looked out the window like I'd seen something interesting. "About what?"

"Your brother? The cops? The arrest? Or maybe you'd like to tell me what you really think about your dad. Take your pick," she said.

"Nothing to say." I hesitated. "Archie's with Dave. He's trying to get a bail hearing set." I sighed and looked at her. "They won't let me see him, Rusty."

I saw Dave's face, how he was when they took him

away. It looked like they'd sucked the life out of him. I chewed on my lip and forced myself to keep talking. "And Mom's worried about Gran and the restaurant and . . ." Rusty leaned forward toward me. If I wasn't careful, I was going to lose it. I couldn't do that. My eyes ran around her room until they hit several sheets of white paper taped up on the wall with Rusty's handwriting on them.

I cleared my throat. "What's that?" I asked, trying to change the subject.

Rusty sat back and swiveled so she could see where I was pointing. "It's a timeline. For the case." It looked like a giant spreadsheet. She'd written down everything that had happened—Sneider's meeting with Dave, when I got to the restaurant—then colored in the corresponding time.

"You did all that?" I asked.

"Yeah . . . I've left space so we can add more. . . ." Her voice trailed off.

I didn't know what to say. "Thanks," I mumbled.

Rusty swiveled back around and picked up the envelope we'd found in Sneider's room. It was still in the plastic bag.

"Now we can add whatever's in here."

"You haven't looked?" I asked.

"Nope. I lifted the fingerprints—one set—Sneider's, I assume, but I didn't peek, honest."

I looked at the envelope. I hadn't had much of a chance to check it out back in Sneider's room. Not enough time. Not that there was much to see. It was standard stuff. A regular-size business envelope. On the front was written one word in red ink: *Traitor*.

"That's his writing. Sneider's," I said. "I recognize it from the note I found in his pocket." I reached over to my backpack and pulled out the note to show Rusty.

She tossed me a pair of plastic gloves.

"More gloves? Buy the jumbo pack?" I said, forcing a smile.

She rolled her eyes. I flipped the envelope over. It wasn't sealed. I opened it and looked inside. A photo. I pulled it out gingerly, like it might break.

"Isn't that . . . ?" asked Rusty.

My heart skipped a beat. "A picture of my dad? Yeah, it's him," I said. I didn't recognize the picture. He was standing in front of a building with two other men. I didn't recognize them, either. Why did Sneider have a picture of my dad? I stared at it more closely.

I flipped it over. On the back was written one word: *Sapphire*. The writing was Sneider's.

Rusty cocked her head to one side. "Sapphire?"

I shook my head. "No clue." My brain buzzed with questions. What was Sneider up to? And what did Sapphire mean?

I set the photo down. I'd hoped the envelope would give us some answers. But it looked like all we had were more questions.

MONDAY

CHAPTER XVII

After dinner, Rusty and I headed back to her room. We talked for hours about the photo I'd found hidden in Sneider's motel room. We didn't get anywhere. When I finally crashed on the couch around midnight, Rusty was still at it. I was exhausted but couldn't sleep. I kept thinking about Dave and Sneider and wishing Mom were home.

I must have dozed off, because the next thing I knew, Rusty was shaking my arm.

"Come on . . . we've got stuff to do," she said.

I fumbled for my watch. It was only six thirty. "Give me five," I mumbled. I pulled on some jeans and met Rusty back upstairs. Her room was command central. The desk, which wrapped around two walls, was covered with stacks of newspapers. I picked up the top copy. It was yesterday's *Santa Fe Ledger*. There was a front-page photo of Sneider on it. My heart skipped a beat as I looked at his face. He was smiling, happy. He looked like a nice guy. Now he was dead.

I dropped the paper back onto Rusty's desk.

"Could you turn that on?" she asked, pointing to an electric hot pot. I flicked the switch and listened as the water started to rumble. Rusty yanked open a desk drawer and pulled out a jar of instant coffee. She shoveled heaping spoonfuls into two mugs.

"Don't tell Mom," she said, pointing at the cups. "She thinks coffee is up there with red meat and palm oil."

I took a sip and winced. "Don't worry. This is not coffee."

"While you were dozing, I've been busy." She spun around in her chair and hit a couple of keys on her computer. Seconds later, pages spewed out of the printer.

"What is it?" I asked, leafing through the sheets.

"Background on Sneider. He is—I mean was—kind of cool. Well, cool in a dweeby science way. He worked for *Particle* for almost twenty years. He wrote about nuclear energy, atomic science—that kind of stuff. All scholarly pieces, except for the one on your dad."

I glanced at the *Particle* home page she'd printed off, then a bio on Sneider. "Can I keep these?" I asked.

She shrugged. "Sure."

I placed them in my plastic folder. "Something's been bothering me. About Sneider, the murder," I said. "Is it okay . . . ?" I pointed to an easel with a pad of paper on it.

"Sure." She tossed me a marker.

I drew a rectangle. "Here's the back kitchen." I sketched in the rear entrance, walk-in fridge to the right and the prep table in the center of the room where I'd first seen the blood. "Now we keep our knives here on a magnetic wall rack." I slid my finger to the left of the room and made an *X*. "Everybody uses these knives, so they're covered with loads of fingerprints. We have a knife service that comes every couple of weeks. They take away the old knives for sharpening and leave us with a new set."

"Right . . . ," said Rusty. I could tell she wasn't sure where I was going with this.

"But Dave didn't keep his knives there." I quickly sketched in the corridor that ran from the far end of the back kitchen to Dave's office, then the main kitchen, and finally the dining room. I pointed to the office. "He kept his knives in a knife roll in his desk. Nobody used Dave's knives but Dave."

"So only Dave's fingerprints would be on them? Is that what you're saying?"

"Yeah. Plus, think about it. If Dave was the murderer, why use his own knife? Why not just grab one of the knives from the rack in the back kitchen?"

"Yeah," said Rusty. "And didn't you say the police found the knife dumped in the garbage outside Chez Isabelle? He wouldn't be that stupid."

I nodded. "So say for a minute that someone else murdered Sneider. Only they don't grab the closest knife either. They go all the way to Dave's office and pick out one of his. They use it and dump it where they know it will be found."

I waited for Rusty to tell me that I was crazy, but she didn't. "Dave didn't freak out and kill Sneider, did he?" she said. "It wasn't payback for the story Sneider wrote about your dad. The murder was planned, calculated."

"Cold-blooded," I added. "I can't prove it, but I don't think Dave killed Sneider. I think whoever killed Sneider knew exactly what he—or she—was doing."

And what they wanted to do was frame my brother for murder.

CHAPTER XVIII

I should have felt better. I was sure Dave was innocent. That was the good news. But it wasn't enough, was it? Rusty read my mind.

"We need proof," she said. "The police have the murder weapon with your brother's fingerprints all over it. All we've got is a theory."

She was right. Detective Suarez wasn't going to drop the charges against Dave based on our big ideas. Plus, I still didn't know why Sneider had been meeting Dave in the first place. I stared at Aaron's photograph on the front page of the *Santa Fe Ledger*. *Why were you here?* I wondered. I leafed through my plastic folder and pulled out one of the pages. Then I picked up Rusty's phone.

"What are you doing?" she asked.

"What time is it on the East Coast?" I asked.

Rusty looked at her desk clock. "Two hours later, so it's nine o'clock," she said. She looked at me quizzically.

"I'm calling *Particle*. See if I can find out what Sneider was working on."

"Just like that?" she said. "You're going to ask and they're going to tell you?"

I found the "contact us" telephone number at the bottom of the *Particle* home page that Rusty had printed out. I punched in the number.

"Sure, why not?" I said. I tried to sound confident, but she was right. I didn't have a plan. Not really. "I'll tell them . . ." I hesitated.

Rusty smirked. "Whatever you tell them, make it snappy. We've got to leave for school in ten minutes— fifteen at the latest."

The line was ringing. I spied the stack of newspapers on her desk. I needed inspiration fast.

"*Particle* magazine. How may I direct your call?" answered a nasal voice.

I froze.

"I—I—"

Rusty snickered.

"I'm sorry, I'm having trouble hearing you. Can you repeat that?"

"Sorry," I said. "I'm calling from the *Santa Fe Ledger*. It's about the murder of Aaron Sneider. Could I speak with someone who worked with him, please?"

"You'll want Jake Whitetower. I'll see if he's in yet."

I shot Rusty a triumphant look. She smiled and shrugged.

"Jake Whitetower," said the voice on the other end. Hard to tell, but he sounded youngish, maybe late twenties.

"Yes, uh, Mr. Whitetower . . . ," I fumbled.

"Jake, please. And you're . . . ?"

My stomach flipped. *My name?* I couldn't give him my real name.

"Hello? You there?" said Jake.

Rusty arched her eyebrows and gestured with her hands. *What's your problem?* she was saying. *Do something.* For a split second I thought about using her name, but that was too weird. My eyes flew past her and did a quick circuit of the room. When they landed on her computer I blurted out, "Mac. Mac Macintosh."

Rusty covered her mouth to keep from howling. I gave her chair a shove and turned away.

"Well, Mac," he said, "how can I help you?"

I sucked in some air before continuing. "I wanted to

ask you a couple of questions about Aaron Sneider." I tried to make my voice sound deeper, more confident.

"Let me stop you there," he said. "I spoke with someone from your news desk before." I heard him rifling through a bunch of papers. "Yeah . . . here it is . . . some guy named Burke called on Saturday."

"Yes . . . well, I'm following up on a few things."

"Let me guess. Burke's too busy to call, so he gets an intern to do his work. Am I right?"

I decided not to argue. Intern sounded a whole lot better than eighth grader. "Yes," I said. "Sounds like you know the drill."

"Mac, I feel your pain. I was an intern once too. But I've got to warn you, I can't say much," he said. "I'm working this story myself. I'm writing a major piece on Aaron's murder and how it's tied to the Keiller spy story. I'm already in discussions with the *Post* and the *Times* for serialization."

"But there's not a definite connection, is there?"

"Come on, Mac. Journalism 101. There's got to be. Too much of a coincidence otherwise. I'm not big on coincidences, are you? So ask away, but no promises."

"Sure. I gotcha. I just wondered what Aaron was doing in Santa Fe. . . . I mean, was he here on vacation?" I asked hopefully.

"Aaron take a vacation?" Jake snorted. "I can't remember the last time he took a day off. That is, unless your idea of a holiday is a physics conference."

"So he was here for . . . ?"

"Mac," he interrupted, "I hate to give you a hard time, but what's in it for me? I mean, if I tell you what Aaron was working on, then what do I get in return?"

"I—I don't know what you mean," I stammered.

"Quid pro quo . . . I tell you something, you tell me something. Surely you've heard *something*. Santa Fe's not that big a place, is it? What's the word on the streets about the murder? And this guy Dave Keiller? You know him?"

I almost choked. "Yeah . . . I know him."

"And . . . ?"

"Well . . ." I paused. "I actually know his brother better." I heard Rusty's chair spin around.

"Younger brother, right?" I heard Jake shuffling some more papers. "Here it is. Austin? That's him, isn't it?"

"Yeah . . . but he goes by Oz."

"Sounds like you know him pretty well," Jake said. I had his attention.

"You could say that."

"I'm listening." He was interested.

I was about to do something that was either incredibly

brilliant or really dumb. Only one way to find out. "We're tight," I said.

"How tight?"

I paused but not for long.

"Tight enough that he'd probably talk to you if I told him to." There. Done. I heard a small gasp from across the room. Rusty. The line was silent for a second.

"Well, that changes things," Jake said finally. He was serious now. "I'd like to talk to him. A lot." He paused, then added, "You think you could arrange that?"

Sweat broke out on my face and down my back. How was I going to pull this off? Arrange an interview with myself? It didn't matter. I'd figure that out later.

"Yeah. I think so, but I'll need a couple of days."

"The sooner the better."

I wiped my face on my shirt. "I'll do the best I can."

"I need better than that, Mac. I'm trusting you on this. You'll keep your end of the bargain, right?"

"Yeah, of course," I said. "But what about Aaron? What was he working on?"

He paused for a second before saying, "Aaron was writing a book."

"A book?"

"Yeah, on the Keiller spy story. It was based on his

original piece, plus some new research he was doing. Or so he said. That was all I could get out of him. He was pretty tight-lipped about the whole thing." I was so stunned I couldn't say anything.

"Mac? You there?"

"Yeah, sorry," I stammered. "Just taking some notes."

"He said he'd be in Santa Fe for a week and would explain everything when he got back. Only he didn't. Get back, I mean."

"So no idea what the new research was?" I managed to say.

"No, but I'm sure it's all on his computer. And his computer belongs to *Particle*, so we'll know as soon as the police release his things."

A book? I couldn't believe it. Aaron was writing a book about my dad. I couldn't think of anything to say.

"Here, let me give you my cell phone number," he said. "Call or text as soon as you speak to the brother, okay?"

"Sure," I mumbled. "This book . . . Aaron was really serious about it?"

"Aaron was always serious." He chuckled. "He even had a title for it."

"Really?" I choked out.

"Yeah . . . he said he was going to call it *Traitor*."

CHAPTER XIX

"You promised him *what*?" Rusty said.

"You heard me. I told him I'd get him an interview."

"With Oz Keiller. Who—last time I checked—was you. Or are you Mac Macintosh now?"

I rolled my eyes. "Hysterical, Rusty. I didn't have a choice, did I? Plus, I found out what Aaron was working on, didn't I?"

Rusty shrugged. "I guess. And now we know why Aaron wrote the word 'traitor' on the envelope we found in the motel room."

I picked up my coffee cup, then set it back down again. The coffee swirled in my stomach like battery acid. A book about my dad . . . my dad the traitor.

"Now that Aaron's dead . . . do you think they'll still publish it?" I was almost afraid to ask it.

"Sneider's book?" asked Rusty. "Hard to say. I guess it depends how far along he was. But come to think of it, it might be even more popular now that Sneider's dead."

"Any more good news?" I asked. I stared at the coffee cup. I needed to eat something. When *was* the last time I'd eaten?

Rusty looked over at me. "Oz, I know you don't want to hear this, but the whole book thing gives the police more evidence against Dave. Circumstantial, but it still goes toward establishing his motive."

"How do you mean?" I glanced over at her.

"Just think about it. Your brother finds out this journalist is in town, writing a big expose on your dad. Dave freaks out and kills him to stop the book. It's simple."

"Thanks. You've made me feel so much better."

Rusty tried to smile. "It's not all bad news. I had an idea. You know the picture, the one we found in Aaron's room?"

"Yeah . . . ?"

"Can I borrow it?"

"It's all yours," I said. I handed her the envelope with the picture.

She placed the photograph on her scanner. When she caught me looking at her, she gave me a smile. "You'll see. Just an idea I've got."

I glanced at my watch. We had to leave for school in about thirty seconds. "Great," I said. "I'll grab my stuff while you solve the mystery."

Rusty grunted. She was glued to her computer screen and didn't even look up when I left.

CHAPTER XX

I heard the whispers as soon as I walked into school. I wasn't paranoid. Okay, maybe a little, but who wouldn't be after everything that had happened? Everyone knew some guy had been knifed at Chez Isabelle. Everyone knew my brother did it. They even knew my dad was a spy. Some of them avoided me like I'd killed Sneider myself. The rest pumped me for details. I wasn't sure which freaked me out more.

When the bell rang for lunch, I jumped up and raced out of class. Rusty and I had agreed to meet in the library. When I walked in, the librarian gave me a funny look— I'm not a regular. I made my way to a bank of computers in the back.

"About time," Rusty said without looking up from the computer screen.

In front of her was the photo of my dad and the two other men.

"Do you have to show the world?" I whispered.

Rusty craned her neck around. "News flash. We're the only ones here, okay?"

"Sorry," I muttered. "Bad morning."

I pulled up a chair and sat down next to her. She slid the photo in front of me. "What do you see?" she asked.

"See? My dad. He's on the far left. The guy in the middle looks Hispanic. Maybe midthirties? The one on the right with the thick black glasses is older. He and my dad look about the same age. Not sure . . . maybe early forties?" I looked over at her.

"That's it? That's the best you can do?"

"What is this, a test?" I snapped. "What am I supposed to see?"

She huffed. "The building behind them. See what's written on it?"

I looked at the photo more closely. "LANL."

"LANL. Short for Los Alamos National Laboratory. Where your dad worked. I see the signs all the time when my parents go there for no-nukes protests." She pointed to the two men. "So they must have worked with your dad," she said.

"How does that help?" I asked. She had this way of making me feel like an idiot. Today I wasn't in the mood.

"We don't know who these two guys are, but someone must," she said. "Then I had this idea. There are gazillions of blogs and websites about Los Alamos."

"Sounds fascinating," I said.

She caught my sarcasm and scowled. "Los Alamos is serious, Oz."

I held up my palms. "I can tell," I said.

She ignored me and ticked off on her fingers. "One, it's one of the only labs in the U.S. doing classified nuclear weapons research. Two, it's one of the biggest employers in New Mexico. Three, it has a lot of enemies—like my parents—who want to see it shut down. And four, it has a history of security problems. Your dad's case wasn't the only one."

I sat up when I heard the last one. "Really?"

"Yeah, really. Los Alamos is a hot topic. And that means a lot of people are talking about it in cyberspace. So I chose four different websites and posted the picture."

"And you think someone out there is going to spot the

picture and tell us who these two guys are?" I said.

"That's the idea," she said. She pointed to the screen.

Looking to track down some old LANL buddies.
Anybody keep in touch with these guys?
—High Altitude

"'Old LANL buddies'? What's that about?" I asked.

Rusty's face reddened. "I had to make it sound like I used to work there . . . you know, so they'll write back."

"So who is High Altitude?" I asked.

"That's me, idiot. I had to create a user name, didn't I?"

"Yeah, okay. Any luck?" I said.

Rusty's face fell. "Not yet." She hesitated; then the corner of her mouth turned up. "Someone did say he thought they were alien abductees."

I laughed. Rusty jabbed me in the ribs. It felt like I hadn't laughed in years.

"Now what?" I said.

"We wait." She glanced at her watch. "You want to grab some lunch?"

"You go ahead. I'll catch up with you."

Rusty gave me a funny look but didn't push it. When

she was gone I did a quick circuit of the library until I found what I was looking for. There was a whole section on Los Alamos. I stared at the shelves blankly for a minute.

"I'd suggest you start with this one."

I spun around. It was the librarian. She pulled out a book and showed it to me.

"It's a good introduction to Los Alamos and the history of the atomic bomb." She leafed through it until she reached a photo. "Here's Robert Oppenheimer, the man who headed up the Manhattan Project." She flipped a few pages further. "And the Trinity site in southern New Mexico where they tested the bomb. And there's some Cold War and post–Cold War information too." She looked up at me. I half expected to see a smug look on her face. *You know, some dirt on your traitor dad.* But it wasn't there. Just a smile.

I tried to smile back. "That's great."

I checked the book out.

"I hope you find what you're looking for," she said softly as she handed the book back to me.

Me too.

CHAPTER XXI

Rusty was sure someone would recognize the two guys in the picture. I wasn't, but it couldn't hurt, could it? She checked the computer a couple of times between classes and texted me with updates. Nada. Nothing. During assembly she passed me a page she'd printed out. More bogus postings. This time I didn't laugh. What were we going to do now? I was out of ideas. I was sure the photo was important—why else would Sneider have hidden it in his motel room? I wondered if I should have given the photo to Suarez. Maybe he could have figured out what it meant. I tried to imagine that conversation. No way. Besides, I wasn't even sure Suarez would take it seriously.

After school, I found Rusty back in the library.

"Rusty, look . . . we've got to . . ." I stopped talking. She was staring at the computer screen.

She pointed to it and smiled. "Success."

I sat down next to her and read it.

Hey, High Altitude. Where have you been, man? Siberia? David Keiller died. Don't recognize the guy in the middle. A. J. Powell left the lab back in the nineties. Think he's got a place in Santa Fe. Good luck.

"A. J. Powell?" I asked. "So the guy with the glasses on the right is named A. J. Powell?"

"Looks that way," said Rusty. "I checked the White Pages on the Net but no A. J. Powell."

"Unlisted?" I said.

"Maybe. So I did a public records search."

"Can you do that?" I said.

"If you had the cash, we could even pull up a credit report and find out if he's got a criminal record."

"I'll stick to the phone number," I said.

"See, that's the problem. I found four A. J. Powells. But none of them had phone numbers. I can keep trying, see if I can find another site . . . ," she said.

"Have you got addresses for the four A. J. Powells?" I asked.

"Just a sec." Rusty hit the print key. She pulled a sheet out of the printer, circled four names, and handed it to me.

"You got an idea?" she said.

"You up for a road trip?" I asked.

"You're not . . . ," she said, but she was smiling.

"I am. Let's go meet Mr. Powell."

"Just like that?" Rusty said.

"Sure, why not?" Half of me was serious. The other half hoped she'd tell me not to do it.

"Fine," she said, crossing her arms.

I waited, hoping she'd get cold feet, but she didn't. A thought crossed my mind. We were betting A. J. Powell knew something that would help us find Sneider's killer. What if he didn't? Another dead end. But what if he did—then what? My mind raced. What if Powell was somehow involved in Sneider's murder? Crazy? Maybe, but I had this weird feeling.

Anyway, it was too late to change plans. Rusty wasn't backing down, and neither was I. For better or worse, we were going to find A. J. Powell.

CHAPTER XXII

Let's go meet Mr. Powell. Seemed simple enough when I said it. We only had four A. J. Powells to check out—how hard could that be, right? Wrong. An hour later we'd met Amelia Jane Powell (in her eighties, single, ten cats), aj Powell ("lowercase, please, and no periods between *a* and *j*," she said), and some guy in his twenties who slammed the door in our face.

We were down to the last Powell. He—or she—lived on Calle Cabrillo. On the map it looked pretty straightforward. Take West Alameda. Turn onto North El Rancho Road. Then all we had to do was find Calle Cabrillo.

We were fine until El Rancho went vertical. The paved

road ended suddenly and turned into a pockmarked dirt road. After a hundred yards, we gave up trying to cycle and got off our bikes.

Rusty insisted she knew where we were going. I knew we were lost.

She stopped to check out a street sign, then peered at the map. "Should be the next right," she said.

"Are we still in Santa Fe?" I asked. It was hot. I was thirsty, and this was a really bad idea. "I mean it, Rusty. Are you sure you know where you're going?" I said.

Rusty pursed her lips and shot me a frosty look. "Would you like to navigate?"

"Me? Not when you're doing such a great job."

I was so busy talking that I almost missed the sign. There it was: a bent metal street sign that said CALLE CABRILLO.

It didn't look like anyone had lived on sunny Calle Cabrillo for a long time, that is, unless you counted the burned-out car. The piñon and chamisa were so over-grown that I couldn't see a mailbox, let alone a house.

Rusty kept looking around, refusing to admit defeat. If Powell *had* lived here, he'd either moved away or died. Rusty pointed off to our right. "There . . . over there . . . it looks like a path."

"You've got to be kidding," I said. There wasn't a sound except for the wind rustling in the trees and our voices. No cars, no people, nothing. We'd passed the last house a quarter of a mile ago. But somehow it didn't feel like we were alone. It felt like someone—or something—was out there.

Rusty headed down the path. Reluctantly, I followed. We ditched our bikes by a tree.

"Come on," Rusty said. "I'm sure this is it." She ran ahead like she'd gotten a second wind.

She reached a clearing, turned, and shouted, "There's the house! I knew it." She shot me that smug look I hate. "Hurry up."

"I'm coming, I'm coming," I said. I swept aside a massive spiderweb and stepped into a small clearing. Up ahead was a rusted chain-link fence. I was about to take another step when I heard a noise. Rusty lifted the latch on the gate. She must not have noticed the noise . . . too busy gloating, I guess. But I did. There it was again. A motor revving or . . . ?

"Rusty, hold on," I said. It wasn't a motor . . . it was growling, wasn't it? I started to run toward her. "Rusty, wait . . ."

A voice shouted, *"ATAQUE!"*

From the corner of my eye I saw a German shepherd hurtling toward Rusty. Its fangs were bared; it was snarling, its hackles raised.

"Rusty, look out!"

Her head jerked up and she saw the dog. But it was too late. She was already halfway through the gate. She was still holding the latch, but she didn't move ... couldn't move.

"Shut the gate, Rusty. Shut it! *NOW!*" I screamed.

Blood pounded in my ears. She wasn't moving, and the dog was racing toward her. I had to get there first.

I sprinted as fast as I could. One step. Another. There. I grabbed the back of her shirt in my hands. I yanked as hard as I could, pulling her and the gate. The gate clanked shut. I reached over and flipped the latch down.

"Get back!" I shouted to Rusty. I looked up. The dog was almost at the gate. For a second I thought we were safe. But one look at the dog and another at the gate and I knew we were toast. The dog would sail over it, no problem. I could see him settling down on his haunches to make the jump when the voice called out again.

"*BASTA!*" he shouted. As soon as the dog heard the command, he stopped, then trotted away from us in the direction of the voice.

I turned back. Rusty was sitting crumpled on the ground.

"Rusty," I said. I was panting heavily, and my lungs burned. I knelt down beside her. We had to get out of there—now. "Are you . . . are you all right?" I asked.

She nodded but didn't say anything. I took a quick look around.

Rusty had been right. There was a house straight ahead of us. Adobe with a red tin roof. A banged-up Chevy pickup was parked on the side. No sign of anyone. Where was the dog? And where had the voice come from?

"Rusty . . . we've got to get out of here . . . can you . . . ?"

Rusty sat up straighter. "I think I'm okay. Just give me a second."

But we didn't have a second.

The gate creaked open. A shadow fell over us. My heart stopped. We weren't alone. I turned my head slowly. Work boots. Faded blue jeans. Coming toward us.

"Don't move," the man said. His voice was gravelly and deep. He stepped through the gate, the German shepherd by his side. The dog let out a low growl. He was on a leash now, but I knew with one click he'd be loose. "I'd stay right there, if I were you."

I took another look at the dog and nodded. We weren't going anywhere.

CHAPTER XXIII

His hair was gray and his unshaven cheeks sunken, but it wasn't hard to recognize A. J. Powell from his picture. He even had on the same black glasses, only now one of the arms was held on with a strip of masking tape.

"Mr. Powell?" I asked. My heart was pounding, and my body was shaking all over.

"Who wants to know?" he demanded.

"I can explain," I said. He didn't move, so I didn't either. "My—my name is Oz Keiller. I think you knew my dad, David Keiller?"

Powell's eyes narrowed to slits. He looked like he wouldn't mind letting his dog finish us off. But then he saw something that made him change his mind. "Keiller?

David Keiller's son? My God," he said. He looked like he'd seen a ghost. "I don't believe it. I should have recognized you immediately. You're the spitting image of him." He shook his head slowly.

"Uh . . . Mr. Powell . . . your dog . . . is he . . . you know . . . ," I said. I nodded my head toward the dog.

Powell looked at the dog like he'd forgotten it was there. "Rio? He's fine now, aren't you, boy?" He gave the dog a pat. The dog wagged his tail. "Good guard dog, especially living out here. I don't get many visitors. Keep myself to myself, if you know what I mean."

I stood up slowly. I turned and helped Rusty up. She had a couple of scratches on her arm, but she looked okay. "This is my friend Rusty," I said.

"Hope Rio didn't frighten you," he said.

"He's quite a guard dog," I said, trying to smile. Rusty shot me a look, but I ignored her. We needed Powell's help.

Powell smiled and nodded. "Can't take the credit. Got him from a DEA agent. He got him off a gang of drug runners. Rio guarded their drugs. They're the ones who taught him the commands."

"Impressive," I said. I cleared my throat. "We're really sorry to bother you, Mr. Powell. We would have called, but we couldn't find your phone number."

"Don't believe in 'em. Phones, that is. Never have. No one I want to talk to," he muttered. "So why are you here, anyway?"

"This," I said, fishing the photograph out of my backpack.

He shot me a quizzical look. "Better bring it over to the porch so I can take a proper look," he said.

Rusty and I followed Powell across the yard and up three steps to a narrow porch that ran the length of the house. His hand trembled slightly when he held the photo. He motioned to some metal chairs. We sat down and watched as he looked at the picture. I snuck a quick look at Rusty. *You okay?* I mouthed. She nodded. I looked back at Powell. I did the math and figured he was in his fifties, but his face was so wrinkled, he looked more like seventy.

He tilted his head and peered at us over his glasses. "Where'd you get this?" he asked. His voice was edgy, sharp. His eyes darted between Rusty and me. I thought about Rio and jumped in.

"We were cleaning out some old boxes, and I found it with my dad's things." His eyes scrutinized me . . . looking . . . looking for what? I held his gaze and added, "See, I never knew my dad. I thought it might help . . . I don't know . . . maybe help me to learn about him."

The words sounded lame even to me. I wished I had another story, but it was the best I could come up with. The question was, would it convince Powell? I watched his face. I was pretty sure he wasn't buying it 100 percent. But if he thought I was lying, he didn't call me on it.

"Hmmm...yes...well, I don't know what to say. Your dad and I started at Los Alamos the same year. That's us in front of the lab where we did a lot of our work."

"What about the other man?" asked Rusty.

Powell shook his head. "Couldn't say. No memory for faces. Besides, there were thousands of guys who worked at Los Alamos back then." He gave me a half smile and started to hand the photo back to me.

"What about the inscription on the back? Does that mean anything?"

Powell flipped the photo over and read it. Was I wrong or had he gripped the photo tighter? I scanned his face, searching for any hint that he knew something. It was blank.

He licked his lips, then shook his head again. "Sorry, but I'm afraid that's a no too." He handed me the photo and stood up, indicating we were done. Either he didn't know or he didn't want to talk. Either way, it was clear we weren't getting any more information.

"I'm sorry I can't help. See, your dad and I worked together, but we weren't close."

He must have sensed my disappointment. "Don't get me wrong. For what it's worth, I liked him, your dad," he said. "A good man. Shame what happened—a real shame. But it's all ancient history. Best focus on the future. Now if you don't mind . . ." Was it my imagination or was Powell in a hurry to get rid of us? "Watch your step on the way out. We get a lot of rattlers out here."

Rusty's eyes darted quickly from the porch to the path.

"We will, and thanks," I said. What a joke. We'd found A. J. Powell, but so what? We weren't any closer to finding Sneider's real killer. Plus, it was more than that. I hadn't told Rusty, but I had hoped Powell would tell me about my dad . . . what he was like. Stupid, I know, but I couldn't help it.

Walking back to our bikes, Rusty and I were quiet. I thought about Powell. I felt sorry for him. In the photo he looked young and happy. Now he was a wreck.

It made me wonder what Dad would have looked like if he were alive. Powell had said I was the spitting image of him. Did that mean that one day I would look like he did in the photo? Somehow, thinking that

I looked like my dad made me feel closer to him . . . something I'd never felt before.

I smiled—I don't know why. I turned quickly to wave good-bye. The sun was low in the sky, and it blinded me for a second. There was Powell on the porch with Rio, where we'd left them. But something was different. I dropped my hand and my smile faded. Powell was turned away from us, but I could see he was cradling something between his head and shoulder. I squinted and looked again. I couldn't swear, but I was pretty sure Powell was talking to someone on a phone. But that was impossible. He'd just told us he didn't have a phone, hadn't he?

CHAPTER XXIV

"You probably imagined Powell was on the phone," said Rusty. "Even if he was, what's the big deal?" She swiveled her desk chair and faced me. I stared at her for a second. She looked okay. She kept telling me she was okay. But I wasn't. I kept picturing Powell's dog racing toward her.

"Earth to Oz. You there?"

I shrugged. "Yeah."

"Yeah . . . ?"

"I really appreciate your help. But back there at Powell's house . . . you could have been hurt. . . ." I stopped talking. I stared at the white time chart on the wall. I had practiced what I wanted to say on the way back from Powell's, but it wasn't coming out right.

"It was a dog, Oz. A big dog, but still a dog." Her face turned red, and she fumbled with a stack of papers. "And okay, so I freaked. I've never been big on dogs that weigh more than ten pounds." She smirked and glanced over at me. "You won't tell anyone, will you?"

"Your secret is safe with me."

"Besides, it doesn't matter what happened back there," she said. "I'm in this, okay?"

"Yeah, but it's not your problem," I said. I was about to say, *It's mine,* but my cell phone started ringing. I grabbed it from my backpack.

"Hello?" I said.

"Oz? It's Archie. Glad I finally got you. I've been trying to reach you."

"Is everything okay?" I said. "Is Dave all right?"

"Dave's fine," said Archie. "I wanted to let you know about the arraignment."

"When is it?" I asked.

"It was this afternoon."

"Was? It's over? But I wasn't there," I said.

"I'm sorry. I tried your cell, but you didn't pick up. Anyway, arraignments rarely take more than a few minutes. It was over before it started," he said.

"Still . . . ," I said. While I was out chasing A. J.

Powell and a dead end, Dave was in court. I'd let him down. I should have been there. "But everything was okay, right?"

The line went silent. "Oz, I'm afraid the judge denied bail."

I felt like I'd been kicked in the stomach, then kicked again.

"But they can't do that. Dave is innocent."

"I hoped the judge might set bail. Ties to the community, no prior criminal record, that kind of thing. But it was a long shot. Dave is charged with murder. If he's found guilty, he could get a life sentence."

"Life?" I blurted out. "They can't do that."

"Oz, calm down. I didn't mean to upset you. I'm just saying the judge has to take this seriously. He has to consider that Dave might pose a significant flight risk."

"But he didn't do it," I repeated. "Why can't anyone see that?"

"The most important thing is that we get Dave's case ready for trial. In the meantime, I've arranged for you to see him tomorrow at the jail. I've spoken to your principal, and she says it's fine for you to miss some classes. Can you meet me at my office first thing?"

"Yeah," I mumbled. "Whatever."

"Oz, I'm going to do everything I can to help Dave. I spoke with your mom again. Your grandmother is doing better, and your mom is on her way back home. With any luck she should be back in Santa Fe by Wednesday or Thursday at the latest."

I thanked Archie and hung up. I looked over at Rusty. She'd been sitting perfectly still during the phone call.

"Bad?" she asked.

"Really bad," I said.

"Oz, even if he got a life sentence, he could get parole one day."

"Gee thanks, Rusty. That makes me feel a lot better."

"I just meant . . . ," she said.

"Forget it. Let's drop it, okay?"

"Can I do anything?"

"Not unless you know who killed Sneider," I said.

"Not exactly . . . but I did find something," she said. She leaned over. She had two sheets of paper in her hand.

For a moment my heart lifted. Maybe she'd found a clue—something, anything that would help us figure out who'd killed Sneider.

"I just printed it out. Haven't had a chance to read it yet," she said.

I reached over and took the pages from her. I stared

at it in disbelief. "This is Sneider's original article," I said.

"Yeah, I know. Someone from the chat room sent me the link. I can't believe we didn't think about looking for it before."

"Rusty, I've seen this," I said, tossing it onto her desk. "Remember? At the police station?"

"Yes, I remember," she said. The smile left her face. "I thought it might help . . . thought it might have more information in it . . . something you missed the first time."

I was about to say something but stopped myself. This wasn't Rusty's fault. She was trying to help. Plus, she was right. I hadn't read the whole article when I was with Suarez. I'd only glanced at the first couple of paragraphs.

I leaned over and picked the article back up.

Most of the stuff I knew. Sneider talked about my dad, his career, and how he'd stolen the classified documents. I skimmed the rest until something caught my eye. I stopped reading.

I grabbed my backpack and rifled through the two exterior pockets. I found the photo from Sneider's motel room and pulled it out.

Rusty peered over my shoulder at the article. "What is it? What did you find?"

"See that?" I said, pointing to what Aaron had written on the back of the picture: *Sapphire.*

"Yeah?" said Rusty.

I pointed to a paragraph on the second page. "Read that."

It took only a second. Rusty took a deep breath. "Jeez . . ."

I read it out loud, not believing what it said.

> My source insisted on complete anonymity. I
> knew him only by his code name: Sapphire.

"Oz, that's not the only thing. Look at this," she said, pointing to the picture of my dad in the article.

"Recognize it?" she asked. She placed the photo we'd found in Sneider's room next to it. It was the same photo. They'd cropped out A. J. Powell and the third man, but it was definitely the same picture.

"The photo we found in Sneider's room is the one he used in his original article?" I asked.

Rusty nodded her head. "Looks like it."

I flipped the photo over and looked at the inscription again. *Sapphire.* I flipped it back and stared at the two men standing with Dad. "One of these two guys must be Sapphire. That must have been why Sneider wrote it on the back." I stared at the two faces. That meant one of them was Sneider's source, I was sure of it. One of them told Sneider my dad was stealing nuclear secrets.

The question was, which one?

TUESDAY

CHAPTER XXV

Rusty's dad dropped me off on Water Street, a couple of blocks from the plaza. Breakfast was in full swing at Café Pasqual's, but otherwise, the downtown was quiet. I hung a right onto Don Gaspar and wove past a line of people waiting for a table. I nodded to a couple of townies I knew. The smell of hash browns and chili sauce wafted from the café kitchen. I was starving. I glanced at my watch. I had five minutes before I had to be at Archie's office but still not enough time to grab a take-out breakfast burrito. I'd promised Archie I'd be at his office by eight thirty so we could go see Dave.

I took a left onto San Francisco and was about to head up the steps to Archie's office when I stopped. I'd been so busy yesterday that I hadn't had time to track down Carlos. It was still bugging me, what Razor had said. If Carlos and Dave were together after closing on Friday, then maybe Carlos was Dave's alibi. Good news. But it didn't make any sense. If Dave had an alibi, why hadn't he told the cops? And where was Carlos now?

I had to find Carlos. I didn't have his number, but I figured Razor did. It was too early to call, so I texted him instead. CARLOS STILL MIA?

I hit send just as a voice called out, "Perfect timing. I'm parked right around the corner."

It was Archie. I had tried not to think about visiting Dave in prison. I wasn't sure I could handle it. But I didn't have a choice, did I? I couldn't put it off any longer. I followed Archie over to his car, a very cool 1971 vintage 280SL Mercedes-Benz convertible.

As I slid into the passenger seat, my phone beeped. It was a message from Razor. YEP. STILL MIA.

I texted back and asked Razor for Carlos's number. I had to find Carlos. I had to find out what was going on. *Where are you, Carlos? And what were you and Dave doing on Friday night when Sneider was murdered?*

CHAPTER XXVI

SANTA FE COUNTY CORRECTIONAL FACILITY. That's what the sign said at the turnoff from I-25. In case you missed it, they repeated it again in big letters over the entrance.

"I'll drop you off and find a parking space," said Archie as he pulled up to the front.

I didn't say anything, just nodded.

"Oz . . . I know this is tough. Just hang in there, okay?"

I nodded again. From the outside, the building could have been a school, but the CCTV cameras and uniformed guards gave it away. On my way to the entrance I tried Carlos's cell. There was no answer, so I left a message.

I took a deep breath and headed into the building. I tried to psych myself up . . . tell myself I needed to be tough . . . look positive for Dave.

The tough guy thing went out the window when I saw Dave behind the thick glass barrier in the visitors' room. The guard pointed to a hard metal chair at a booth and walked away. Dave looked bad—really bad. His face was thin, and he'd aged about a hundred years. The thing that hit me was how scared he looked. I'd never seen Dave look scared before.

I sat there for a second, struggling to think of something to say. Finally I mumbled, "You—you okay?" Dave motioned to a phone on the left-hand side of the booth. I picked up the receiver and repeated what I'd said.

"I've been better," he said. "You should be in school. I don't want you missing school."

"It's okay. Archie talked to the principal." I didn't tell Dave that school was the last place I wanted to be.

"How's your hand?" I asked, pointing to his bandaged palm.

"Hurts, but it's okay," he said.

"What . . . what happened?"

"Stupid mistake," he said. "I was doing prep for the weekend after we finished on Friday. I wasn't paying attention and cut myself." Dave was lying. He never cut himself. He never made a mistake. Never lost his focus.

I started to say something, but he interrupted me. "Forget my hand. It doesn't matter. We don't have long. I need your help. Archie spoke with the police and they said you can reopen the restaurant tonight."

He said "you" and not "we." I traced a divot on the table with my finger. "Are you sure you want . . . ?" My voice trailed off. The thought of Chez Isabelle without Dave . . . no way.

"Oz, we don't have a choice. We can't afford to stay closed. Every minute, every day we're shut . . ." He didn't finish the sentence, but he didn't need to. "Razor already knows, but I need you to help. Do you understand?"

"Yeah . . . okay . . ." We were both silent for a moment, then I said, "Dave, I've got to ask you something." I scoped out the room. There were a few people—moms, girlfriends, lawyers—talking to prisoners. A couple of guards were standing around, but they looked bored, like they'd seen it all before.

"I . . . I found a note . . . the other day at Chez Isabelle," I said.

Dave looked at me blankly.

"A note? Oz, what are you talking about?"

I heard a bit of the old Dave. Exasperated . . . ticked off.

"It was about a meeting at the restaurant Friday night . . . really Saturday morning."

Dave cocked his head. His forehead furrowed. "What . . . ?"

"The note. Sneider wrote it . . . the guy who . . . you know . . ." I leaned closer and lowered my voice. "It was about a meeting with you."

"What? Are you sure?" he said. He shook his head and said, "That doesn't make any sense."

"What doesn't make sense?" I asked.

He looked up, like he'd forgotten I was there for a minute. "Nothing. Never mind. Do the police know about the note? Did you show it to them?"

"No." I swallowed hard. "I knew . . . I knew it would look bad, so I kept it."

I could see Dave was weighing up everything I'd said. "Oz . . . where did you find the note?"

I shook my head. "It doesn't matter. I just did, okay?"

Dave sighed. "Oz, I don't know anything about a note. Yes, I knew who Aaron Sneider was. His article destroyed our family. I could never forget that." He rubbed his temple. "But I never met him. I swear."

"But then where were you?" I blurted out. "When the

police called, they couldn't find you. And no one can find Carlos. . . ."

Dave's head snapped up. "Forget Carlos. I gave him some time off. End of story."

"But Razor said—"

"Forget what Razor said," Dave said flatly.

"But maybe he can help," I said.

Dave looked away. He gritted his teeth. "This has nothing to do with Carlos."

"It does," I said. "They think you did it. Why don't you just tell the police where you were?"

Dave squeezed his eyes shut but didn't say anything. Finally he muttered, "I can't. It's not that easy. Trust me."

I stared at him. *Trust me?* I didn't know who to trust. Say Dave was telling the truth, then what? Sneider thought he was meeting Dave. Did he meet someone else? I thought about my theory that Dave was framed. Could someone have set up the meeting to get Sneider to the restaurant and kill him? But why?

"Oz? Oz?" My head jerked up. Dave had said something, but I'd missed it. "The note . . . the one you found. Where is it now?" he asked.

"It's safe. I promise." There was something else I had to ask. "Dave . . . when all this stuff happened with

Dad . . . did you and Mom ever figure out who leaked the story to Sneider?"

Dave frowned. "No . . . we never knew. Sneider refused to reveal his source, then Dad died and we wanted to put it behind us. Oz . . . why are you asking?"

"No reason . . . just curious."

A guard stepped over to me. "Visiting time is up." I glanced at Dave. He froze. In a flash I realized he didn't want me to go . . . he didn't want to go back inside. He caught me watching him and cleared his throat.

I wanted to ask him more questions, but there wasn't time. "Dave, I'm gonna find out what happened. I promise I will."

"Oz, don't worry about that . . . but you've got to keep the restaurant going. I need you to do that for me. That's the most important thing."

I stared at Dave for a minute. I wondered if he'd seen the news. Wondered if he knew the whole world thought he was a cold-blooded killer. Wondered if he knew Chez Isabelle was hanging on by a thread. I hoped he didn't. I didn't think he could handle it.

I stood up and looked him straight in the eye.

"I will. I'll keep Chez Isabelle going. I promise." I just hoped it was a promise I could keep.

CHAPTER XXVII

Before I left the prison visitors' room, I made up my mind. I wasn't going back to school. If they hassled me, I'd tell them I'd spent the day with Dave and Archie. I had to get to Chez Isabelle. See if Razor was there. Start doing the prep. Without Dave, we'd be pushed to get everything ready for dinner service. Dave was counting on me, and I wouldn't let him down.

I was so focused on my plan that I didn't notice Detective Suarez until I slammed into him.

"Where are you going in such a hurry?" he asked.

"Sorry . . . I've got to . . ." I was about to tell him I was going to Chez Isabelle. What was I, crazy? Tell him what I was doing? He'd probably arrest me for skipping school.

"Just see your brother?" he asked, but it was more of a statement.

"Yeah," I muttered.

"I'm on my way to see him myself," he said. I looked up. He knew that would get my attention. "Hoping he can help me out with something. Actually, hoping he can help himself."

Now I was hooked. He continued, "We're tying up a couple of loose ends on the case. Always happens . . . there are a few questions you can't answer."

"Like what?" I asked. As soon as I said it, I could have kicked myself. I was playing into his hands, but I couldn't help it. Maybe—just maybe—he was having second thoughts . . . realized Dave was innocent, that someone else had done it. That dream didn't last long.

"Like who helped your brother," he said. "Our crime scene guys are pretty sure that two people were involved."

"Two?" I swallowed hard. I didn't get it. I figured one person killed Aaron. One person dumped the body in the walk-in fridge. One person got rid of the knife.

"It looks like someone held Sneider down while another one stabbed him," said Suarez. A shiver ran down my spine. Suarez's face didn't show anything. It was like he was talking about a bag of garbage instead of a dead man. "If Dave gives us a name, the DA might go easier on him . . . then again, his accomplice might come forward himself . . . realize he's in trouble and give evidence against your brother."

What was he saying? I looked up at him. His eyes were cold and steely—staring at me, accusing me. That's when it clicked. *I* was the accomplice. He thought Dave and I were in this together. He was offering me the chance to pin it on my brother and save myself.

My mind spun back to when I'd found Sneider's body. The blood. How the cop found me trying to run away. Suddenly I saw how it looked. How they thought I was guilty too.

Suarez kept talking. "I hate loose ends, but I figure we'll get this sorted out soon," Suarez said. "Either your brother talks or the accomplice comes forward . . . whoever talks first, wins." He scrutinized me for a second before saying, "You're close to your brother . . . any ideas?"

I had a horrible sinking feeling. I remembered the flashlight I'd left behind in Sneider's room on Sunday. I bet the cops had found it.

Then the sinking feeling got worse. I'd never put the plastic gloves back on after I'd slipped the room key back onto the maid's cart. My prints were all over the flashlight.

Suarez must have known that I'd been in Sneider's room. He was stringing me along and waiting for me to take the fall.

A tiny voice in my head told me to spill. To tell Suarez everything and hope for the best. Another voice interrupted. *Dave's innocent. He didn't do it. And you've got to prove it.*

I ignored the first voice. I had to play this out. I took a deep breath and stared back at Suarez. "Sorry . . . I can't help you."

"Can't or won't?" Suarez said. He ran his hand across his shaved head. He kept looking at me. When I didn't say anything, he shrugged. "That's too bad."

There was nothing more to say. I turned and headed toward the double doors and the waiting room. Suarez's voice rang out after me. "Oz, I'll keep digging till I find out the truth. I won't give up. I never do."

I stopped and looked back at him. "I guess that's something we've got in common then."

CHAPTER XXVIII

I was in a seriously great Mercedes convertible. The sun was shining. I was missing science class. Life couldn't get any better, right? Except for two small details: My brother was in jail charged with murder, and my dad was a traitor.

I hadn't said a word since we'd left the prison. Archie tried small talk. He even gave me a rah-rah speech about how he'd get Dave off. It was no good. All I could think about was Dave stuck in prison . . . the look on his face . . . the fear.

Archie parked his car around the corner from his office. I mumbled something about checking in at Chez Isabelle. I was afraid he was going to hassle me about getting back to school, but he didn't.

"Of course. Let me drop these files off upstairs and I'll give you a ride." He glanced at his watch and scowled. "I didn't realize how late it was. I'll have Helen call to say I'll be late for my next meeting."

"Don't worry about it. Seriously. I can walk," I said, getting out of the car. The walk wasn't long, but I wanted to be at Chez Isabelle now. I'd promised Dave I'd keep Chez Isabelle going. I wouldn't let him down.

"Are you sure?" Archie asked as we headed down the sidewalk.

"No worries." We stopped outside the entrance to his office.

"I'll be in touch, and if you speak to your mom before I do, please have her call me."

Just then we heard footsteps coming down the stairs from Archie's office. It was Harrison Smith, the guy I'd seen talking to the journalists at the police station on Saturday.

"Archie. Just the man I was looking for," he said, walking over and giving him a clap on the shoulder. When he caught sight of me, he turned and arched his black eyebrows. "You're Oz Keiller, aren't you?"

I felt my face go hot. I nodded. "Yes, Mr. Smith."

"Please. Call me Harrison," he said, extending his hand.

"We've met at your family's restaurant before, haven't we?" I nodded. His handshake was firm, and he looked me straight in the eye the whole time. The reporters were right. He was definitely campaigning, and he didn't seem to care that I was too young to vote. He wore a suit and tie with an American flag lapel pin. I looked at him closely. Despite the white hair, he wasn't that ancient. Still in his fifties, I figured.

"Am I interrupting?" He looked from Archie to me.

"No. We're all done, aren't we, Oz?" Archie said.

Harrison's face went serious. "I don't have to ask what you were meeting about, do I?"

I hoped the ground would open up and swallow me. Unfortunately, it didn't.

Harrison kept talking. "Oz, let me say that my thoughts are with you and your family at this difficult time. You know I'm a very big fan of Chez Isabelle. I hope things work out for you all."

I mumbled something that sounded like thanks and studied the sidewalk again, looking for that hole.

Next second, Harrison was Mr. Smiley again. "Now, Archie. I wondered if I could tempt you with lunch at the Compound. My lunch meeting canceled on me at the last minute."

"I wish I could." The Compound is one of the best restaurants in town. I could tell it hurt Archie to turn down the invite. "But I'm actually running late for a meeting. Can I take a rain check?"

"Absolutely," said Harrison. "I'll just have to eat solo."

"Actually, could you do me a favor?" Archie asked. "Oz is on his way to Chez Isabelle. Would you mind dropping him off on your way?"

"Of course not. It would be a pleasure."

"That is, if it's okay with you, Oz?" Archie asked.

"Sure. That would be great."

Not really, but I couldn't complain. At least it was faster than walking. I'd be at Chez Isabelle in ten minutes. And right now, that was the only place I wanted to be.

CHAPTER XXIX

I hoped Harrison would talk about his campaign . . . the weather . . . football . . . anything but the murder. No luck.

"You know, Archie is one of the best attorneys in town. Your brother is in good hands," he said, putting the key into the ignition of his Lexus. It had that new car smell. Expensive but not flashy—the kind of car a politician would drive to impress the voters.

I didn't know what to say, so I just nodded.

"And don't forget reasonable doubt, Oz. That's all it takes." Harrison glanced into the rearview mirror, then pulled onto Water Street.

I turned to look at him. "How do you mean?"

"Other possible scenarios that could explain what

happened to this guy Sneider. All a jury needs is reasonable doubt to find your brother not guilty. Plus, I'm sure he has a perfectly good alibi for the time Sneider was killed."

"Well . . . ," I mumbled.

Harrison shot me a look, then turned back to the road. "I'm sorry. I didn't mean to pry."

"No, it's not that," I stammered. "Dave was home asleep." No wonder the police didn't believe Dave. It sounded lame even to me. I didn't mention that Dave's car was gone when I left for work Saturday morning.

"I see." We were both silent for a minute, then Harrison said, "The funny thing is that I'd forgotten all about Aaron Sneider until I read the story in the paper."

He'd lost me. "I don't . . ."

"The article he wrote. About your dad. I was at Los Alamos when it all came out," he said.

"You worked at Los Alamos?"

"For over ten years." Harrison got into the right-hand lane and turned onto Paseo de Peralta.

"Did you . . . did you know my dad?"

"David? Of course. One of the leading lights at the lab. And just so you know, I thought it was a shame he never had a chance to clear his name. Dying the way he did . . . the whole thing was a tragedy."

"Thanks," I said.

Thinking about my dad gave me an idea. It was a long shot. Rusty said that thousands of people worked at Los Alamos. Still, maybe Harrison knew something.

"The article," I said, "the one that Sneider wrote. Did anyone at Los Alamos figure out who his source was?"

Harrison tapped his fingers on the steering wheel while he waited for a chance to turn onto Canyon Road.

"Interesting question. I do seem to remember a lot of speculation at the time. You know . . . people trying to figure out who Sneider's inside connection at Los Alamos was."

I held my breath.

Smith pulled out. "But nothing definitive as far as I can recall."

"Oh."

"Is it important?"

"I'm not sure. I thought . . ." I wasn't sure what I thought anymore.

"Even if you did figure out who the source was, there's a good chance he's not working at the lab anymore. It was what—thirteen or fourteen years ago? There's a big turnover, plus a lot of layoffs. He might even have died," he said.

"Here we are." He pulled over to the curb outside the front entrance to Chez Isabelle.

I grabbed my backpack and opened the car door. "Thanks for the ride. I really appreciate it."

"Any idea when you're reopening?"

"Tonight," I said.

"Good to know. You can expect to see me soon," he said.

"Thanks. And thanks again for the ride."

"You're welcome. And Oz," he said, leaning toward me. "Don't forget what I said. Reasonable doubt. That's all it takes."

CHAPTER XXX

I watched Harrison's car pull away. I turned and stared at the empty restaurant. I'd been in a rush to get to Chez Isabelle, but now I wasn't so psyched. I wasn't sure I could handle going inside, back where the murder happened. I pulled out my phone. Maybe I should call Rusty or try Carlos again. But I didn't. I clicked it shut. The calls could wait. I had to get this over with, and the sooner the better.

At least Harrison had dropped me off at the front entrance. Going in the back door would have been too much. Too many memories of Saturday, when I'd found Sneider's body. Not like I needed reminding. Every time I thought about Chez Isabelle, I thought about Sneider. I hadn't told anyone—not even Rusty—but I kept picturing him, slumped in the walk-in fridge, surrounded by blood. It was worse at night when I tried to sleep. But it wasn't much better during the day.

I slipped my key in and gave the door a shove. The air was warm and heavy, and a thin layer of dust covered the tables. Chez Isabelle had been closed only a couple of days, but it felt like a hundred. If Mom were here it would have been all right, but she wasn't. It was just me.

I shook my head. *Snap out of it*, I thought. *Remember what Dave said. He's counting on you.* I took a quick look around. "Razor?" I called. No answer. I took a deep breath and headed down the hall. Past the kitchen. Past the office. My heart beat faster. I paused for a second, then stepped into the back kitchen.

As soon as I did, there was a loud *whoosh*. I froze. The walk-in fridge door swung open. Images of Sneider—his body, the blood—flashed through my mind like a movie. But then I saw him. It was Razor. I heaved a sigh of relief.

"Jeez, you scared me," I said.

"Scared *you*?" he said, laughing. "How about me?"

Razor shifted a stack of fruit and vegetable boxes onto his hip and closed the walk-in door. "You're early. Bagging school?"

"Just visited Dave. Figured you could use the help. Besides, school . . ."

"Not your favorite place?" I shook my head no. "If it makes you feel any better, it wasn't mine, either." He set the boxes on the prep table. "So Dave . . . how was he?"

"Bad . . . really bad." I looked over at Razor. "I've never seen him like this."

Razor frowned and tugged at the red bandanna tied around his head. "I'm not surprised. This is serious stuff."

"Yeah, but Razor, he didn't do it."

He held up both hands. "I'm not saying he did. We all know Dave's got a temper, but *kill* a guy?" He shrugged. "Not that anyone would blame him after what that guy did to your family. But it's not me you've got to convince, it's the cops."

My face fell. "I know . . . but he's innocent. I've got this feeling. . . ."

Razor shook his head. "Oz, I've had run-ins with cops before and trust me, feelings are one thing they don't have. Besides . . ." Razor's voice trailed away.

"Besides what? What is it?"

"It's just . . ." Razor paused. There was something he wasn't telling me.

"Come on. What is it?"

"It's probably nothing." He met my eyes. "I stopped by El Farol after work on Friday. On my way home, I saw lights on here."

"Here? At Chez Isabelle?"

Razor nodded. "There was a car in the parking lot. I thought it was weird and was about to call Dave and let him know."

"But . . . ?"

"But I didn't." Razor frowned. "Because it was Dave's car. I recognized the CIA bumper sticker a mile away."

"So he closed on Friday," I said. "Big deal."

"Oz, it was after we closed. Must have been around midnight."

My stomach lurched.

"I've been going over it in my mind a thousand times, trying to figure out what Dave was doing here," said Razor. "We closed by eleven. When I went to say bye, he was in his office with the door closed. I could hear Carlos and him talking."

"Did you tell the police?" I could hardly get the words out.

"No . . . not yet. I've been trying to figure out what to do," said Razor.

"Razor, you can't tell them."

"Oz, I can't cover for Dave. I can't lie to the police."

"No . . . I don't mean that. I mean, don't tell them unless they ask, okay?"

Razor shook his head, his eyes closed. "Oz, this is serious stuff. If I don't tell them, then I could be in big trouble too. And it's not like I've got a squeaky-clean record as it is."

"Please, Razor. Dave didn't do it. I'm sure. Someone framed him. They wanted to make it look like he did it. I'm going to figure out who did it, but I need more time. Just don't say anything to the cops for another day or two."

"I don't know, Oz." Razor stared at me like he was trying to make up his mind. "Okay, here's the deal. I won't say anything, but if they ask, I won't lie. Got it?"

I smiled. "Got it. Thanks. I really appreciate it."

Razor stuck his hands up in the air to stop me. "Subject closed." He dropped his hands to his sides. He drummed his fingers on the vegetable box before looking back up at me. "Oz . . . I know Dave's your brother. You want to believe he's innocent. I want to believe he's innocent too, but . . ." I started to interrupt, but Razor jumped back in. "All I'm saying is that we both have to be prepared that wanting him to be innocent doesn't mean he is."

I tried to swallow, but the lump in my throat wouldn't

budge. I knew Razor was right. But I also knew that if I started to think Dave was guilty, it was all over. I couldn't go there.

Razor let out a sigh, then smiled. "Enough of the heavy stuff," he said. He lifted up the vegetable box and set it on his shoulder. "We've got work to do. Can you grab the whole salmon from the second shelf and the box of herbs?"

"Sure. No problem."

I watched Razor walk away toward the front kitchen. I took a deep breath and tried to stop shaking. I thought about what he'd said. He wouldn't say anything about Dave's car, at least for now. But what if he changed his mind or the cops started asking him questions? Bottom line? I didn't have much time to prove Dave was innocent. I only hoped I had enough.

CHAPTER XXXI

"I think we could both use some Zep," said Razor. He cranked up the stereo, and a loud guitar riff filled the room. I set the salmon and the herbs down on the counter in the front kitchen.

"Should I work in the back? Get the vegetables prepped?" I asked, pointing to the prep area by the sinks.

"You're up here with me tonight."

My jaw dropped. Razor laughed and gave me a crooked smile. "Close your mouth—you're attracting flies."

I'd never worked up front. I was always in the back, peeling potatoes, washing lettuce, scrubbing pots. If I was lucky, Dave let me cook the family meal for staff before service. It was grunt work, but Dave said that was how chefs got their start.

"We're so short staffed it will be a miracle if we don't get slammed," Razor said. "I need you up here cooking with me."

"Yeah, but . . . ," I mumbled.

"You know the recipes," he said, turning back to the counter. He selected a chopping board and looked over at me. "So, no buts, okay?"

I tried to convince myself it was no big deal. I found an apron, fired up the ovens, and gave a chef's knife a couple of strokes on the steel. I'd seen Razor and Dave do this stuff a thousand times but still, this was different—this was real. At first I kept glancing over at Razor to make sure I wasn't screwing up, but he'd only nod and keep singing along with Led Zeppelin.

After a while, I stopped looking at him. Everything faded away except the food in front of me. Razor called it the zone. When I glanced up at the clock, it was nearly five forty-five p.m. I couldn't believe it. The whole afternoon had flown by. This was my dream—I was a real cook. I imagined what everyone would say if they could see me now—Mom, Dave, Rusty . . .

Rusty . . . My smile faded. I'd promised to call her after I saw Dave.

"Earth to Oz, you there?" said Razor.

"Sorry," I said, shaking my head. "I need to make a quick call. Is that okay?"

He looked at his watch. "Make it fast."

I whipped off my apron and jogged down the hall. First I called Carlos, but still no answer. By now I was used to getting his answering machine. I left another message. Then I hit Rusty's number.

"Hi. It's me," I said when Rusty answered.

"You're alive. Good to know. Any idea how many times I called you today?"

She didn't wait for an answer.

"No? Well, about a million."

"Sorry. I'm really sorry. I went to see Dave, then I came straight to the restaurant. But guess what? I'm cooking tonight, with Razor."

"Wow. That's great news." The sarcasm was heavy.

"Rusty, I talked to Dave," I said, hoping I could pull her off the ceiling. "He didn't know about the note I found on Sneider. He said he'd never met Sneider. He didn't know anything about a meeting. I'm sure he's telling the truth. Dave's a lousy liar."

"Unlike you," she said, but I could tell she was smiling.

"Somebody else killed Sneider and they're framing Dave. I'm sure of it."

I heard Razor clear his throat. I turned around. He was standing in the doorway. He motioned his head toward the front of the house.

"First covers are here. You ready to rock 'n' roll?"

I nodded. "Rusty, I've got to go. I'll tell you everything when I get back."

"How are you getting home, Einstein?" she said. "Your bike is here."

"Dunno. Guess I'll get a ride with one of the guys."

"I'll see if Dad can pick you up. And Oz . . . one thing . . ."

"Yeah?"

"Try not to poison anyone."

It was slow at first, but by seven o'clock we were jamming. The kitchen was open plan, so guests could see everything we were doing. No swearing and no dropping pans was Dave's mantra. Razor and I worked on a long stainless-steel prep table that faced the dining room. In front of that was a big oak table where servers opened bottles of wine and sliced loaves of sourdough bread. Behind us was the stove and salamander for grilling. A row of blackened but clean sauté pans hung from butcher's hooks on a pot rail that ran above the stove so we could grab them easily. There wasn't much space, so Razor and I were in a constant dance, sliding pans under the grill, plating food, and handing it off to the servers.

"Two duck, one skate-no-capers, one coq," Razor called out when a server handed off the first order.

"Firing two duck, Chef," I said, slipping the duck breast into a sauté pan.

"Oz, do me a favor."

"Yes, Chef?" I called back.

"Drop the Chef, okay?"

"Yes, Ch—I mean, Razor."

During a lull, I checked out the dining room. It was totally different from this afternoon. It sparkled, and there was a buzz. It wasn't packed but it wasn't bad—I mean, considering everything that had happened. Razor and I figured a lot of them actually came because of the murder. We even found one guy trying to take a photo with his cell. Sick but true.

Razor caught me surveying the dining room, watching them eating, laughing, sipping their wine.

"There's nothing like it, is there?" he asked, smiling. "I

mean, what other job is there—legal job—where you can make people this happy? It's crazy."

He was right. It was crazy, and I realized I never, ever wanted to do anything else.

By ten o'clock things were winding down. The last tables ordered dessert, and Razor and I started to break down our station.

JoJo, the maître d', poked his head into the kitchen. "Good job, guys," he said.

It was all I could do to smile back. Every muscle in my body ached. It was okay while we were cooking, but once we stopped I realized how tired I was. I was never here this late, especially on a school night, but now it was different. No Mom, no Dave, and we hadn't stopped at all. We'd eighty-sixed the duck, and there were only two skate wings left. I wrapped up what was left and stacked the hotel pans in a bus bucket.

"Here," Razor said, tossing me a bottle of water. I unscrewed the top and gulped the whole thing down. "It's late. Why don't you head out? I'll lock up."

I started to protest, but he was right. I grabbed my backpack and jacket from Dave's office. On the way out I caught Razor chatting up two girls at one of the tables.

Classic Razor. He was always doing the rounds and schmoozing the customers. I called out good night, but he didn't hear me. Outside, the air was incredibly cold. I stood for a second sucking it in, trying to clear my head. Car lights flashed in the parking lot.

"Oz, over here!" It was Rusty's dad. He waved, and I waved back. I said a silent *Thank you* to Rusty for dealing with the ride.

"Boy, am I glad to see you," I said, hurrying over to the car.

"Good night?" he asked as we pulled out of the parking lot.

"Yeah," I said. It had been a good night. Not perfect, but good. Tomorrow I'd do it all over again. I'd try to do it better. I'd keep doing it until Dave got out of jail or Mom got home . . . until they didn't need me anymore. At the back of my mind, I wondered how long I could keep it up. I pulled my coat around me and closed my eyes. I already knew the answer to that question: as long as I had to.

WEDNESDAY

CHAPTER XXXII

"Did you find out how Dave hurt his hand?" Rusty asked. We swerved through a crowd of students on their way to class. I'd slept through most of my classes and was gulping down a soda for the caffeine hit.

"He said he cut himself doing prep after service on Friday."

"Do you believe him?"

"Is it important?"

"Might be. It's not uncommon for an assailant to get injured during a knife attack."

I smirked. "It's not uncommon? You've been on one of your crime websites again, haven't you?"

Rusty frowned. "This is serious, Oz. It could be

another piece of evidence against Dave."

"Only one problem. Dave's not—what did you call him?—an *assailant*. I keep telling you he didn't do it."

Before I knew what was happening, Rusty had swung around and shoved my shoulder against a locker.

"What are you doing?" I shouted. I caught a group of kids staring at us. I lowered my voice. "Have you gone mental?"

"Just listen, idiot," she said. "Dave stabs Sneider." She thrust an imaginary knife at me. "Hits bone." Her hand jerked. "Dave's hand slips and bam—the knife slices his hand." She let go of my shoulder and walked ahead.

I caught up with her. "Okay, I get your point. It's just hard to explain. . . ."

"Try me," she said.

"Dave is a pro with knives. I can't remember the last time he cut himself." Rusty started to say something, but I jumped in. "But that doesn't mean he cut himself . . . you know . . ." I didn't say *killing Sneider* but we both knew that was what I meant. Something wasn't right. I knew that. But I didn't know what.

Before Rusty could say anything my phone rang. I dug it out of my jacket pocket. Razor's name flashed up on the screen.

"Hey, Razor," I answered. "I'll be at the restaurant as soon as I can. I've only got one more class."

"Slow down. That's why I called. I'm glad I caught you before you left."

A horrible feeling swept over me. "Why . . . what is it? What's wrong?"

"It's . . . I don't know how to say this." The line was silent for a moment. "Oz, we can't open tonight."

"What do you mean? We've got to open." My mind raced.

Razor stopped me short. "Oz, there's not enough staff. We've got a bunch of no-shows, and I can't get any of my buddies to pinch-hit."

What was he saying? They'd refused to come to work? I couldn't believe it. It had to be a mistake. "What about Carlos and JoJo . . ." My voice trailed off.

"I still can't find Carlos, and the others . . . well, they're freaked out," said Razor.

I thought back to last night. Everyone had been more serious than usual, but so what—who wouldn't be? But walk out? I couldn't believe it. I felt sick. Then I thought about Dave and I felt worse. I'd promised him. We had to stay open no matter what.

I blurted out, "Okay, then we do it—me and you.

We were great last night. We'll do it again."

I heard him sigh. "It's not enough, Oz. Think about it. No waitstaff, no prep cooks, no pastry, no dishwashers—it won't work. Besides, reservations have been canceling right and left. Even the curiosity seekers don't want to eat here anymore."

That hurt, but I didn't say anything. A lump filled my throat, and I couldn't swallow. Maybe I shouldn't have been surprised. I knew things were bad, but not like this. For one second, a wild thought zipped through my head. I'd do it myself. With or without Razor. It only took another second to realize I was out of my mind. There was no way I could run a restaurant on my own.

"Oz? Oz, you there?"

"Yeah . . . I'm here." My voice cracked. I fought to keep it together.

"Oz, it will be okay."

Razor kept saying that, but it wasn't okay. He didn't believe it, and neither did I. And once we closed, there was no guarantee we'd ever open up again.

"Oz, I gotta go. Give me a call later, okay?"

"Yeah, later," I mumbled. The only thing that could save Chez Isabelle was proving that Dave didn't kill Sneider. All I had right now was a bunch of theories.

I thought about my promise to Dave. I'd let him down. I'd let Mom down. I'd let everyone down. If I couldn't keep this one simple promise to keep Chez Isabelle going, then how was I ever going to keep my bigger promise . . . to find Sneider's killer?

CHAPTER XXXIII

"Two fish tacos and one shrimp, please," I said.

"Black beans or pinto?" asked the guy behind the counter.

"Black."

"And for the young lady?" he said, indicating Rusty.

Rusty was still reading the menu. After Razor had called to say Chez Isabelle wouldn't open, I lost the plot. I sat through my last class like a zombie. Luckily, my teacher didn't call on me. Not that it mattered . . . nothing mattered now. Rusty suggested grabbing something to eat at Bumble Bee's Baja Grill. I think she hoped it would take my mind off things.

"What do you want?" I asked her.

She looked up. "Uh . . . I'll have the . . ." She scanned the menu board.

"Today, please."

"How about the Fiesta Platter?" she said finally.

"Rusty, that's for eight people," I said.

"I'm hungry," she moaned.

I turned back to the guy and said, "She'll have the Burrito del Norte."

"With chicken," she put in.

I paid, and we sat down at a school-bus yellow Formica table in the back. Black and yellow bumblebee piñatas dangled from the ceiling, and mariachi music played. I set our order number on the table and grabbed two glasses of water.

"Chips, please," Rusty said. She plopped down in a plastic chair.

I filled up two bowls from the salsa bar with tortilla chips and a container each of green tomatillo sauce, *pico de gallo*, and roasted tomato salsa. I brought them back to the table. After we'd hoovered the tortilla chips, Rusty came up for air.

She pulled out the photograph of my dad, A. J. Powell, and the third man and placed it on the table. "So what have we got?" she said, picking at the last tortilla crumbs from the bowl.

I touched my fingers to my thumb to make a zero. "Nada," I said.

She rolled her eyes. "Not true. We know this is A. J. Powell," she said, tapping him with the tip of her knife. "Is he Sapphire? Don't know. Could be."

"Okay, I'll play," I sighed. "Powell definitely knows more than he let on." I shrugged. "Maybe we should go back there . . . see if we can get more information."

"I don't think he's talking. And if he is Sapphire, it's probably not a great idea."

Rusty was right. I was grasping at straws.

"Fish and shrimp tacos?" said the waitress. I nodded, and she set them down in front of me.

"And Burrito del Norte with chicken," she said. "Anything else?"

"I think that's it. Thanks," I said.

She turned and was about to go when she stopped. She was staring at the photograph. Great. I'd forgotten to cover it up when she came over. Now it was too late.

"What are you doing with that?" she said, pointing at the picture. She'd gone from friendly to frosty in about thirty seconds.

"Uh . . . ," I said, scrambling. Rusty always said stay close to the truth when you're lying, so I did. "It's a picture of my dad. He's the one on the left. The other guys worked with him."

She eyed me suspiciously.

I decided to try for the sympathy vote. "My dad died before I was born," I said.

I looked at her but couldn't tell if it was working. I took a chance. "Do you know them?"

"Just the one in the middle," she said slowly. "His name was Victor Martinez."

Rusty caught my eye. "*Was?*"

"He's dead too," she said. "Many years."

"How long?" I asked.

The waitress stared into space for a moment as she did some mental arithmetic. She shook her head. "Over ten years ago."

Rusty caught my eye again. *Around the time my dad died.* Something buzzed in the back of my brain . . . something Harrison Smith had said in the car yesterday . . . what was it?

The waitress smiled. "He was such a handsome man. Linda would love to see this," she said, pointing at the photo.

"Linda?" Rusty said.

"Victor's wife."

I jumped in. "Does she live around here? I'd be happy to take it by. You know, let her take a look."

She looked surprised.

"It would be nice to meet someone who knew my dad," I added quickly.

The waitress smiled. "Sure. I haven't seen Linda in years, but she'll remember me. Tell her Rosie sent you."

"We will. Thanks, Rosie," I said.

I looked at the man standing between my dad and A. J. Powell. *You're Victor Martinez. The question is, are you Sapphire?*

CHAPTER XXXIV

It didn't take long to find Linda Martinez's home. Rosie had written the address on the back of a napkin. It was a small adobe on a postage-stamp-size piece of property on a street off Agua Fria. A double metal swing stood in the front yard, and terra-cotta pots filled with red geraniums lined the front porch. Not big. Not flashy. But neat, like the person who lived there cared.

The sign on the gate said CUIDADO CON EL PERRO. "I'd better go first," I said, "in case it's an attack dog like Powell's."

Rusty smiled. "What, like that one?" She pointed to the front porch, where a tiny fur ball sat. As soon as we opened the gate, it came barreling down the walk. When it got within a foot of us, it stopped and rolled over on its back.

Rusty knelt down and scratched the dog's belly. "Thanks for saving me from this one, Oz."

"Hysterical, Rusty. Absolutely hysterical." I brushed past her, walked up to the front door, and rang the bell. Heels clicked toward the door. Silence. Must be checking us out in the peephole. Finally a metal bolt slid open, then another one. The door opened but just a crack. There was a chain on it. This place was like Fort Knox. A woman peered out at us.

"Yes?" she asked.

"Mrs. Martinez?"

"Who are you?" she asked.

She wasn't making this easy, was she? I gave her my "I'm as trustworthy as a Scout" smile.

"My name is Oz—Austin—Keiller. This is my friend Rusty." I told her about Rosie and the photo I had of her husband and my dad.

"We could show you, if . . . ," said Rusty, motioning toward the door. Mrs. Martinez stared at us for a moment, then shut the door and slid off the chain. If I thought she was going to invite us in for milk and cookies, I was wrong.

Without a word, she took the photo. I looked at her

while she looked at it. Midforties, I'd say. Nicely dressed, and she had a rock on her hand that looked like it weighed a ton. Matching pair of earrings, too.

She gave the photo about ten seconds, then thrust it back like it was toxic.

"I'm not sure why you're here," she said. Defensive? Angry? Whatever it was, it wasn't good.

"Well, see, I never knew my dad, and I thought—"

"I never met your father," she interrupted. "He worked with my husband Victor, but that was years ago." She glanced past us as if she were expecting someone.

"We understand from Rosie that your husband died around the time my dad did," I said.

"I wouldn't know anything about your father's death," she snapped.

"Oh no, it's not that. It's just . . ." My voice trailed off.

Mrs. Martinez smoothed her dress and pursed her lips together tightly. "Victor died over thirteen years ago in a car crash. An accident," she added quickly. "A terrible, terrible accident. Now, if you don't mind, I'm afraid I'm quite busy."

"Of course. I'm so sorry. You've probably just gotten home from work," I said.

She shot me a quizzical look but didn't say anything.

Before she could shut the door in my face, I said, "I don't suppose I could use your bathroom before we go?" I gave her an embarrassed look. She sighed, then opened the door reluctantly.

"I suppose. But I really am in a hurry. Down the hall on the right." She didn't move. Probably wanted to make sure Rusty didn't try to steal the geraniums.

I scanned her house quickly. Nicer inside than out. A lot nicer. In the hall there was a table with photos in silver frames. Living room had a gigantic-screen TV and enough electronics for a small country. Marble counters in the kitchen and a professional-style stainless steel oven and refrigerator. One last look, then I dashed into the bathroom. I flushed the toilet and turned on the water for effect. Back down the hall.

"Thanks. I really appreciate it," I said to Mrs. Martinez.

She gave me a look that was more scowl than smile. She mumbled something that might have been "good-bye." I'd barely hit the front steps when the door slammed behind me.

"Get the feeling she was glad to see us go?" I asked Rusty as we walked down the path.

Rusty smirked. "Big-time. But why? And what's with all the locks?"

I shook my head. "I think she's scared," I said, opening the gate.

"Scared?" Rusty said. "Of what?"

I closed the gate and looked back at the house. A curtain twitched. Mrs. Martinez was watching us. "Not what . . . who. And that's what we've got to find out."

CHAPTER XXXV

Rusty and I were about to jump on our bikes when we heard a voice.

"Now, isn't she Miss Popular these days."

I looked around but couldn't see anyone.

"Excuse me?" I called out.

A head peeped over the fence next door to Mrs. Martinez's place. It belonged to a tiny woman who was about a hundred fifty years old. She had a white nimbus of hair that was bigger than her head. She was wearing pink polka-dot gardening gloves and holding a pair of gardening shears.

She chuckled. "Your friend, Mrs. Martinez," she said.

"She's not our friend . . . ," I started to say.

"Never one for visitors, then all of a sudden it's like Grand Central Station," she continued. She covered her mouth in mock horror. "Now, where are my manners? My name is Rosemary Compton."

I walked my bike over to her fence. Rusty followed. I told her our names. "What did you mean about visitors?" I asked.

"I don't think I've seen anyone come in or go out of that house since her husband died. Well, except for her son, of course."

"Mrs. Martinez has a son?" Rusty asked.

"Oh, yes. Victor Jr. is at Yale studying medicine. Harvard undergraduate. Very bright boy."

Made sense. One of the photos on her hall table had looked like a graduation shot.

"So recently she's had more company?" Rusty asked. Something was bothering me, but I wasn't sure what.

"I'll say," she said. I tried not to crack a smile. I had a feeling Rosemary didn't miss anything that happened on this block. "A few days ago a man came to visit her. Stayed quite a while, if I remember correctly."

"You don't happen to remember what he looked like, do you?" I asked.

She wagged a finger at me. "Now young man, there

is nothing wrong with my memory." She beamed. "In his fifties, I'd say. Slightly plump. Nicely dressed. I like a man who cares about his appearance, don't you?"

My heart beat faster. I fished around in my backpack and pulled out a piece of paper. I showed it to Rosemary. "It wasn't this man by any chance, was it?"

Her face lit up like she'd just won the lottery. "Why yes, it was. Do you know him too?"

Rusty glanced at the paper, then over at me. Her eyes were big. "I don't believe it," she said under her breath.

"Believe what, dear?" asked Rosemary.

"Oh, you know . . . what a small world it is," I said. I folded the picture of Sneider and slipped it back in my backpack. Sneider had visited Mrs. Martinez. And now Mrs. Martinez was scared. Was it something Sneider said?

"And now look," chirped Rosemary. "Here's the other gentleman who came to call. It's like a party, isn't it?"

I turned just in time to see a man getting out of a car halfway down the street. It couldn't be, could it? *It was.* Had he seen us? Didn't look like it. He was busy getting something from the backseat.

I spun back to Rosemary. "I'm sorry, but we've got to run. We're going to be late for dinner."

"Oh, now, that's too bad," said Rosemary.

I caught Rusty turning to look behind us. "Don't," I whispered. "Just ride." I gave a quick wave to Rosemary. Now my heart was really racing.

"Lovely to meet you both," Rosemary called out. "Do call again!"

I pumped hard. Rusty caught up with me. "What was that about?" she demanded.

"Hang a right."

"Oz! What is going on?" Rusty asked.

"There was a man back there."

"Yeah?"

"I know him."

"You *what*?"

"It was Archie McCallister, my brother's lawyer."

"Your brother's attorney is visiting Linda Martinez?" Rusty asked.

"Looks like it." Archie was on his way to see Linda Martinez, and if Rosemary was right, it wasn't the first time. The only question was, why?

CHAPTER XXXVI

Rusty and I found an empty park bench along Alameda. Some kids zipped past on skateboards.

"Okay, let me get this straight," said Rusty. "Victor Martinez died in a car accident around the time your dad died."

"According to Mrs. Martinez."

"Why would she lie?"

"I'm not saying she did, but I didn't exactly trust her, did you?" I said. "Plus, where did she get the money for all that stuff?" I told Rusty how her house was decked out with the latest everything. "Did you see how she looked when I mentioned work? There's no way she has a job. Plus, her son went to Harvard, then Yale. That's big money."

Rusty shrugged. "Maybe she got an insurance payout or sued someone when Victor died. And her son could be on a scholarship."

"Maybe, but I don't think so."

Rusty twisted around to face me. "What I don't get is what Archie was doing there."

I sighed. That had been bugging me, too. "I can't believe it's a coincidence, can you?"

"What? That Sneider visits Mrs. Martinez, turns up dead in your restaurant, then Archie pays her a visit?" asked Rusty.

"Don't forget that Archie takes on my brother's case, too," I added.

"Don't worry, I hadn't. You know where it leads us?"

"Sneider."

"Sneider," Rusty repeated. "It's all connected—it's got to be."

I didn't say anything for a minute. There was something there. Something about Sneider—who he was and what he was up to. I racked my brain trying to find the thread. Finally I said, "Remember what Sneider said in his article? You know, about Sapphire?"

We'd read the article so many times that Rusty recited it from memory. "'My source insisted on complete anonymity. I knew him only by his code name: Sapphire.'"

"'*I knew him only by his code name*' . . . Sneider never met Sapphire, did he?"

Rusty furrowed her eyebrows. "But if they never met, how did Sneider get the info for the article? Smoke signals?"

"Dunno. Phone calls? E-mail? Did they have e-mail back then?"

"Hmm . . . probably fax or something like that," said Rusty. She paused for a second, then said, "No . . . not fax. They wouldn't risk it. Definitely phone. But that still doesn't explain why Sneider visited Mrs. Martinez."

"What if he wasn't looking for her?"

Rusty shot me a puzzled look.

"What if he was looking for Victor?" I said. Slowly it dawned on me. "What if he was really looking for Sapphire?"

"I don't get it," Rusty said. "He thought *Martinez* was Sapphire?"

"Or Powell. I bet Sneider visited Powell, too, or he would have if he hadn't been killed. Maybe Sneider was trying to figure out which guy in the picture was Sapphire."

"Like us . . . like we're trying to do," said Rusty. "But why? Why after all this time?"

I waited for a minute, then said softly, "Because he realized he'd gotten it wrong . . . that my dad didn't do it."

Rusty's head snapped up. "Oz, don't go there. I understand that you want to believe your dad was innocent, but this is crazy."

"Is it? Is it crazy? All I know is, Sneider was in Santa Fe for a reason. Someone didn't like it and killed him." I drummed my fingers on the bench. "I wish we knew more about this book, the one Sneider was working on."

"You asked Jake what's-his-name, didn't you?"

"He didn't know much."

I thought back to the conversation I'd had with Jake, trying to remember everything he'd said. There was something there, too, I knew it. My heart beat faster. I looked at Rusty.

"When I talked to Archie, I asked him what he remembered about Sneider . . . that night at the restaurant. He said Sneider had a laptop with him. When I spoke to Jake at *Particle*, he said something like, 'We'll know more once we get his computer back.'"

Rusty's eyes brightened. "You think the answer is on Sneider's computer? Whatever he was working on would be there, wouldn't it?" Her face clouded over again. "But the police have the computer, don't they?"

"Do they?" I said. "I don't know. But that's what I'm going to find out."

"How?"

"Let's drop by Archie's office."

"But Archie's at Mrs. Martinez's."

"I know," I said. "That's what I'm hoping."

CHAPTER XXXVII

We locked our bikes and took the stairs to Archie's office two at a time.

"I'm afraid he's out at a meeting," Helen, his personal assistant, said when I asked if Archie was in.

I tried to look disappointed. "Gosh, I was hoping to speak with him. Any idea when he'll be back?"

"Let's see . . ." She scrolled down her computer screen. "Hmm . . . I'd guess another half an hour or so. But you never know. Do you want me to have him give you a call?"

"It's kind of important. Is it okay if I wait?"

She gave me a smile. "Of course. Make yourself comfortable."

I looked at Rusty. "Is that okay with you?"

"No problem," she said. "I think I'll run over to the library. There's a book I want to check out."

I gave her a wave and parked myself in a chair. I flicked through some boring law journal. What a snooze. Every ten seconds I glanced at my watch. Finally I heard footsteps tearing up the stairs.

The door flew open. Rusty raced in, panting like she'd done the fifty-yard dash in record time.

"What's wrong?" Helen asked. "Are you all right?"

Rusty grabbed on to the desk like she was about to pass out. "What kind of car does Archie drive?" she asked me.

I sat up straight. "A Mercedes, why?"

"White?" Rusty asked.

"Yes," Helen said. There was a hint of panic in her voice.

"It's just when I was outside I saw some kids hanging around a car. Looked like one of them had a set of keys. A lot of cars have been keyed lately, so . . ."

Helen jumped up. "I thought he took his car," she said. "He didn't say where the meeting was, but I assumed—"

"Maybe he walked?" I put in.

"I'll be right back," she said. She was out the door in a flash.

I felt bad for not offering to help, but I got over it.

"Come on," Rusty whispered. "We don't have long."

We ran into Archie's office.

"What are we looking for?" I asked.

"Files on your brother's case."

The office was filled with stacks of file folders. The phrase "needle in a haystack" came to mind.

I flicked through a couple before I realized that each stack was a separate case.

"Over here," called Rusty. "It's got to be one of these." She pointed to a stack of five or six folders. She split the stack in two and handed half to me.

"What am I looking for?" I asked.

"An evidence log."

I darted a quick look out of the office, but it was still quiet. I started flipping through the top folder. "Translate into English, please?"

She didn't look up from her stack. "A police report that lists everything they found in Sneider's motel room."

I flipped through the first folder. Nothing. I put it back onto the stack.

Rusty tapped her foot impatiently. "We've got to hurry. She'll be back any second now."

"Thanks for reminding me." Second one—nothing.

Same for Rusty. She tossed another folder back into the pile.

"Nothing here," she said.

Two pages into the last folder and I found it. "Got it."

Rusty put the rest of her folders down. She leaned over and peered down at the sheet I'd found.

"Not much, is there?" she said as I ran my finger down the list. Shaving cream, razor, bottle of antacids, aspirin . . .

I stopped and looked up. "Did you hear that?" Footsteps coming up the stairs.

"Oz. She's back. Hurry."

"I'm going as fast as I can, okay?" Magazine, crossword puzzle dictionary . . . Nothing exciting . . . clothes . . . I stopped. There it was. At the bottom of the page. *Computer cable.* I scanned the rest of the list, but no computer.

"Oz. *Now.*"

I turned the page . . . another list, this time for his rental car. It was even shorter . . . a map of Santa Fe, a pack of mints, and some clip-on shades for his glasses. That was it. No computer.

I closed the file and slid it back in with the others.

We both stood up just in time to see Helen come back into the office huffing and puffing.

"Any luck?" I asked. She shook her head as she struggled

to get her breath back. She finally looked up. "What are you doing in Archie's office?"

"Uh, sorry. We just wanted to look out the window...see if we could see what was happening," I said apologetically.

"I couldn't find his car," Helen said. "Are you sure it was his?"

"Pretty sure," Rusty said in her best "I'm not sure at all" voice. "Four-door, right?"

I rolled my eyes. "Rusty, Archie drives a two-door convertible, you idiot." I looked over at Helen. "I'm really sorry."

Helen smiled. "That's okay. Accidents happen. And better safe than sorry."

I shot a glance at my watch. "Yikes. I didn't realize it was so late. We better head out. Will you let Archie know I stopped by?"

Rusty and I left and headed down the stairs.

"Well?" Rusty asked as soon as we were outside.

"No computer," I said. "The police found a computer cable, but a computer wasn't listed. So they don't have it. We didn't find a computer when we searched his room either. Someone else got it."

What was on Sneider's computer that was so important? And who had it now?

CHAPTER XXXVIII

When I left Archie's office, I headed home to pick up some clean clothes. I told Rusty I'd meet her back at her place.

My brain was buzzing. It seemed like every time Rusty and I figured out something, we ended up with ten more questions. It was like trying to follow a recipe with half the steps left out.

I was so busy thinking about Sneider's computer that I didn't notice anything was wrong until I put the key in the front door lock. Chisel marks. I ran my finger along the edge of the door. Someone had jimmied the lock. I slipped the key back into my pocket and listened for a second. It was quiet, but that didn't mean anything, did it? Whoever broke in could still be inside, right?

There was only one way to find out. I gave the door a slight push. I stared into the hall. Empty. Was it? My mind raced. Maybe whoever had broken in was still here, waiting for me.

I stood there, trying to make my heart slow down. I took a deep breath and stepped inside. Silently I slipped off my backpack and set it down by the door.

I edged along the hallway. I stopped. The living room was a train wreck. Someone had gone mental. CDs scattered on the floor. Cushions ripped off the couch. Books everywhere. The kitchen was even worse. Drawers yanked out. Stuff tossed on the floor.

Call the police, I thought. *And tell them what?* Suarez was convinced I was in on Sneider's murder. He'd take one look at this place and figure I'd done it myself to throw suspicion away from Dave and me.

Plus, nothing was stolen, as far as I could tell. TV, stereo, game station—all there. I had a sinking feeling in my stomach. This wasn't a normal robbery. Whoever did this was looking for something special. But what? I couldn't prove it, but I was sure it had to do with Sneider's murder.

I swallowed, trying to get rid of the lump in my throat. I was an idiot. Why hadn't I searched my own home? It was so basic. Maybe there was a clue—another photo, a note—

that might have helped us figure out who killed Sneider.

In a daze, I walked through each room until I reached my room. I hit the lights. I had thought things couldn't get worse. I was wrong.

The pillows were slashed. Feathers and foam covered everything, like a freak snowstorm. The bookcase was knocked over and my cookbooks were everywhere.

My heart skipped a beat. I bent down and picked up *James Beard's American Cookery*. The cover was torn off and the pages tossed around like confetti. It was the first book I'd bought when Mom started paying me for working at Chez Isabelle. I'd found it on eBay and outbid someone else at the last minute to get it.

My hands shook as I gathered up the pages and set them down on my desk. I tried to stop the shaking, but I couldn't. I won't lie. I was scared. Someone had broken into our house. They wanted something. Maybe they found it. Maybe they didn't. Maybe they wanted to send me a message: Back off.

I was getting closer to the killer, but that meant the killer was getting closer to me, too. I clenched and unclenched my fists until my hands stopped shaking. Finally the fear went away. In its place I felt only one thing: anger.

CHAPTER XXXIX

"Did you call the police?" asked Rusty. I was on an empty back road on the way to Rusty's place when I got her call.

"They won't do anything," I said, shifting my backpack. "Suarez thinks I'm Dave's accomplice, remember?"

"Now you sound totally paranoid."

"Can you blame me?" I said. "But it's not just me. Whoever broke into our house probably knows where you live too. Have you noticed anything strange?"

"Besides my parents?" She tried to laugh. "Sorry, not funny. Okay, so I'm getting freaked out. I know you don't want to hear this, but maybe we should call the cops. Let them handle it."

"Can we talk about this later? I'll be at your place in fifteen."

"What did you say?" Rusty said. "This signal is awful."

"I SAID . . . ," I yelled into the phone.

"Just tell me everything when you get here, okay?"

A car crested the hill coming toward me. It was the first car I'd seen in a while. The driver was ignoring the speed limit, like 99 percent of Santa Fe drivers. Probably doing forty in a twenty-five mph zone.

"Oz, did you hear me?"

I glanced up at the car. Why wasn't it slowing down? If anything, it was picking up speed.

"Rusty . . . something's wrong," I shouted.

"Oz—I can't hear you. I'm hanging up."

Click.

"Rusty, I—"

The line was dead. It was too late anyway. The car had crossed the median strip. It was going fast—too fast— and it was heading straight for me.

CHAPTER XL

A couple of tons of metal barreled down on me. No time to think. I jumped away from the car and toppled into an arroyo that ran next to the road. I crashed hard. Pain shot up my arm. I was sprawled in a bed of sand and gravel. Car brakes screeched, and a cloud of dust filled the air. I was alive. But for how long?

Tires spun. The car backed up. They weren't finished. I tried to stand, but I couldn't put any weight on my arm. I rolled over to my other side and clutched my arm. I got up but kept low to the ground. I scrambled toward a stand of piñon trees. It wasn't much cover, and I was an easy target. I didn't stand a chance.

I kept moving. I had to put some distance between

me and whoever was driving the car. A car horn blared. I waited for the sound of a door slamming. Nothing. No one running after me either.

"Are you crazy?" a man's voice shouted. I turned and saw a pickup truck parked on the side of the road. Where was the other car? More wheels spinning. This time taillights flashed. I caught a quick glimpse of the car, then it was gone. I collapsed against a tree to catch my breath.

The pickup truck door opened, and a heavyset man in a cowboy hat and jeans jumped out. "Hold on," he called. "I'm coming down."

He skidded down the slope into the arroyo. "You okay?"

I nodded. "Yeah . . . I think so."

"They could have killed you. Probably drunk." He shook his head. "No right to be on the road. Here," he said. "Grab my arm. Take it easy up that hill."

My bike was where I'd left it. Aside from a bent rim, it looked all right. I was okay too, except for some cuts on my arms and my ankle. I gently moved my arm. It hurt but nothing felt broken.

The guy pulled out his cell and punched in some numbers. After a few seconds he slammed it shut.

"Can't get a signal. We'll have to call the police back

in town," he said. "You good to ride in the truck? If not, I can drive to one of the houses, use their phone. Get an ambulance out here."

"No, I'm okay, seriously. Just a couple of scratches," I said. I told him Rusty's address and climbed into the passenger seat. *No police, either*, I thought. What would I say? Tell them someone was trying to kill me? I wiped my face on my shirtsleeve.

"Not sure the police will be able to do much," I said, fastening my seat belt. "Unless you got a license plate number . . . ?"

He lifted my bike into the bed of his truck. "Nope. Happened too fast."

"Besides, they're probably a couple counties away by now," I added. He walked over to the driver's side and climbed in. "Why don't I call the police when I get back to my friend's?" I said. "I could take your number so the police can contact you."

"Well, I'm not sure," he said. He pushed his cowboy hat back and scratched his forehead. "Best to call 'em right away."

"Sure. It's just, I'd like to get cleaned up," I said. I gave him my best version of an angelic smile.

"'Course. That is, if you're sure?"

"Definitely." No license plate number, but I did know one thing. This wasn't an accident. Someone wanted me dead. But who?

Trying to sound casual, I said, "You didn't get a look at who was driving, did you?"

He flicked off the emergency lights and put the truck into gear. "Not with those tinted windows," he said. "Should make them illegal." He looked over at me as he swung the truck back into the lane. "You don't know who it was, do you?" he asked.

"No," I said. But I was going to find out.

CHAPTER XLI

"They broke into your house *and* tried to run you down?" Rusty asked as she handed me some bandages and a tube of antiseptic cream. "You're having a seriously bad day."

"I've had better. Tell your mom I was skateboarding and fell."

Rusty frowned. "She's the least of your worries. Someone tried to kill you. It's time to wake up, Oz. We've got to go to the police."

"And tell them what? That someone broke into my house but didn't steal anything? Or that a car tried to run me down? There's no way they'll ever believe me."

"But—"

"No. No cops." I changed the subject. "Look on the bright side. At least we learned something."

"Like . . . ?"

"Like, we're on the right trail."

"How do you figure that?" asked Rusty.

"Whoever killed Sneider knows we're getting close. They're getting worried." I was doing my best to sound like I knew what I was doing. The truth was, I was scared. But if I started thinking about that now, I was sunk. I had to keep going no matter what.

Rusty sighed. "Do you want to see what I pulled up on Victor Martinez?" she asked. I nodded. "It's not much. Upstanding citizen. Worked at Los Alamos for about ten years. Then your dad was arrested and we get some more activity." She slid over an article from the *Santa Fe Ledger* that she'd downloaded. I skipped to the part she'd underlined.

> "I've worked with David Keiller for years. There is no way he stole classified documents from this lab," said coworker Victor Martinez of Santa Fe. When asked to explain how Keiller came to be caught with the stolen papers on him, Martinez said, "He was framed. Pure and simple."

I set the article down on Rusty's desk. "I knew it. Do you believe me now?" I said.

"That's not all," Rusty said. She handed me another page.

"What's this?"

"Follow-up story. Initially the police treated Victor's death as suspicious. There was talk that his brake cables had been cut."

"What do you mean, *initially*?"

Rusty frowned. "It's weird. One minute the police are all hot and bothered. Mrs. Martinez even demanded a grand jury investigation, FBI, the works. Then poof—nothing."

"Hold on. What did you say? Mrs. Martinez thought it wasn't an accident too?"

"At first, yes. Then suddenly the whole story died." Rusty slid a third piece of paper over to me. "Buried on the back page. The investigation closed and death ruled accidental."

"But that's ridiculous," I said. I waved the sheets in the air. "He was murdered to make him shut up. Plain and simple. And Mrs. Martinez"—I jabbed at a page—"was bought off. That's gotta be it."

Rusty sighed.

"I'm still thinking you're jumping to conclusions, but . . . ," she said.

"But what?"

"I've been thinking about what you said . . . about your dad being innocent. I'm not saying I agree with you, but if someone wanted to discredit your dad, then accusing him of spying at Los Alamos would be a good way to do it."

She'd lost me. "How come?"

"Everyone's freaked out about nuclear secrets getting into the wrong hands. Most of the stuff from World War II is still classified. Plus, there have been other spies at Los Alamos. A guy named Klaus Fuchs—a high-level physicist—passed nuclear bomb research to the USSR. Then the Rosenbergs, of course . . ."

"Of course," I said, hoping she wouldn't figure out I had no idea who they were.

Rusty scowled. "Accused of espionage. Executed by the U.S. government. Ring any bells?"

I felt my face go hot. "Maybe . . . a few . . ."

"More recently, computer discs disappeared and there were other security problems."

"So if someone wanted my dad out of the way, then this was a good way to do it?"

Rusty shrugged. "It's a theory, Oz. Only a theory."

"Okay, but think about it," I said. "Sneider comes to Santa Fe. He's got a photo of my dad, Victor Martinez, and A. J. Powell. He goes to Victor Martinez's house. Finds out he died mysteriously. So his next stop is A. J. Powell, right?"

"Probably," admitted Rusty.

"Only when we ask Powell about the picture, he acts like he's never seen it before."

"Maybe Sneider was killed before he could visit Powell," Rusty said.

"Or maybe Powell is Sapphire. Sneider tracks him down. Powell freaks out and kills him."

We were both quiet for a minute. "We need something more on Powell," I said finally. "Something that ties him to Sneider. Some way to prove he was Sapphire."

Rusty shook her head. "I've looked. I posted another message but no luck. I can't find out anything about Powell and nothing to connect him to Sneider. I know you don't want to hear this, but even if you prove that Powell is Sapphire, it doesn't mean he killed Sneider."

She was right. I didn't want to hear it. There had to be a connection. Suddenly it hit me . . . something Harrison Smith said in the car on the way back from visiting Dave.

"Harrison Smith said there were a lot of rumors about who Sapphire really was," I said.

"Yeah, so?"

"So maybe one of those rumors was that A. J. Powell was Sapphire. If we can prove Powell was Sapphire, then we'd have another suspect for Sneider's murder. Or at least enough evidence for the police to question him . . ." My head spun.

Rusty scrunched up her face. "It's a stretch. A big stretch. Besides, how are you going to find out if Powell was Sapphire? It's not like you've got the inside track at Los Alamos."

I smiled. "No, but I know someone who does."

CHAPTER XLII

It wasn't hard getting a telephone number for Harrison Smith. Speaking to him wasn't so easy.

I got bumped over to a PA, who made it clear I wasn't getting near Harrison, if she had anything to do with it.

"I'm afraid Mr. Smith is in a meeting," she said when I asked to speak with him.

"Can I leave a message?"

There was a slight pause before she replied, "May I ask what this is in regard to?"

She wasn't going to make it easy, was she? I put on my smiley phone voice and said, "My name is Oz Keiller, and Mr. Smith worked with my father at Los Alamos. I was hoping to speak with him. I promise it won't take long."

She didn't miss a beat. "Mr. Smith is extremely busy. While I'm sure he'd enjoy speaking with you about— what did you say?—your father, I'm afraid he simply won't have time."

"I'll keep it short," I shot back.

"I'm afraid it doesn't matter." She sighed like she realized I wasn't the brightest bulb. "Mr. Smith has a very important press conference tomorrow afternoon. Then he flies to Washington."

Tomorrow? I didn't have much time. I had to catch Harrison before he left town. I needed his help. He had contacts at Los Alamos. I hoped he could find out if A. J. Powell was Sapphire. Rusty thought it was a long shot. I thought it was our only shot.

I put on my nice voice again and said, "I understand completely, but could you make sure he gets the message?" I gave her my cell number and hung up.

Rusty looked over at me. "Any luck?"

I shrugged. "Not sure . . . we'll have to wait and see." I looked at my watch. Five o'clock. I hoped Harrison got the message.

Rusty swiveled around in her chair. "Would you stop that?" she said, grimacing.

"Stop what?"

"Cracking your knuckles—it's driving me crazy."

"I wasn't . . ." My voice petered out. She was right. I *was* cracking my knuckles. I plopped down on her bed and stared at the ceiling. "I'm sorry," I apologized. "It's the waiting. It's making me mental." It was seven thirty and Harrison still hadn't called. I rolled over and read Rusty's time chart for the thousandth time. I kept hoping everything would suddenly make sense. "Did you find out anything about Harrison?"

"Not much. Mostly recent stuff . . . speculation about his race for the Senate . . . very wealthy . . . gives a lot of bucks to charities . . . that's about it. His consulting business deals with nuclear energy, but it's all very hush-hush. Here," she said, handing me a couple of pages from her printer. "I printed out what I could find."

I leafed through them. One was a photo of Harrison at a ribbon-cutting ceremony. Another was an interview in *Business Week*.

"Do me a favor," Rusty added. "Don't let Mom see them."

"Sure," I said, slipping them into my plastic folder. "But what's her problem with Harrison?"

"Everything. According to her, he's Mr. Nuclear. She's convinced he'll build loads of new nuclear power plants and ramp up the nuclear weapons program."

"Could he do that?"

Rusty shrugged. "Anything is possible, I guess. If he got on the right Senate subcommittee . . ."

My phone rang, interrupting her. It was a number I didn't recognize.

"Oz Keiller," I said, answering it.

"Oz, Harrison Smith here. Apologies for calling so late, but I just got your message."

I motioned madly to the phone. "No, this is fine. Thanks so much for returning my call, Mr. Smith."

"Harrison. Please."

"Harrison. And thanks for the ride the other day." I gave Rusty a thumbs-up.

"Not a problem. My PA mentioned something about your dad."

"You know, the other day . . . I asked if anyone at Los Alamos knew the source of the allegations about my dad?"

"Yes?"

"Well, I wanted to find out more . . . about the rumors, I mean."

"I'm not sure I can help you. It was a long time ago." He paused for a second. "Does this have something to do with the charges against your brother?"

I was stuck. I needed his help, but I didn't want to

tell him—or anyone—more than I had to.

"Oz . . . ? I don't want to rush you, but I'm pressed for time, so . . ."

I caught Rusty staring at me. I stared back, searching her face as if by some miracle it would tell me what to do. She tilted her head and looked puzzled, like she wanted to help but didn't know what was wrong.

I made a decision. I took the leap. "Do you know a man named A. J. Powell?" I said it so softly that I wondered if I had said it at all.

"Powell? Yes . . . I think he worked at the lab." The line went silent. "You don't think he was Sneider's source, do you?"

"I think he might be." I waited for him to laugh and tell me I was crazy, but he didn't. I took a deep breath and said, "You see . . . I've got this picture . . ."

"Picture?" he repeated.

"A photograph of my dad with two other men. One of them is a man named Victor Martinez and the other is A. J. Powell. I think one of them was Sneider's source, and Victor is dead, so . . ."

"So that leaves Powell," said Harrison. "I understand." His voice was serious now. "Have you spoken to the police about this?"

"No . . . I was going to. But then I thought it might not be anything." That was a lie, but I figured it sounded better. "I thought if you did know anything about Powell . . ." My voice trailed off.

"Yes . . . I see what you mean. It was a long time ago, but there are folks I can ask . . . see if anyone remembers any rumors involving Powell." He was silent again. "It's late. My day is rather busy tomorrow, but it probably makes sense to meet in person. I'll take a look at the photo and see if I recognize it." I heard him flipping pages. "It would have to be early."

"Early is okay."

"Of course, you've got school, don't you? Well, shall we say seven o'clock?"

"That's great." It was still a long shot, but somehow I felt better. Harrison was plugged in. He would speak to people . . . find out about Powell . . . "Seven o'clock is fine," I said.

"Meet me at my office? Have you got the address?"

"Yeah, I've got it right here. Thanks. See you tomorrow."

I hung up the phone and looked over at Rusty.

"Are you sure you know what you're doing?" she asked.

"No."

But then again, I wasn't sure about anything anymore.

THURSDAY

CHAPTER XLIII

"I'm going with you," said Rusty.

"No way," I snapped. Rusty and I were downstairs in her kitchen. Her mom and dad had just left to meet up with a bunch of people going to Los Alamos for a no-nukes rally.

"It's better this way, believe me." I didn't mean to be harsh on Rusty, but I couldn't help it. I hadn't slept at all last night. I shoved a bowl of soggy cereal away from me. No appetite.

Rusty crossed her arms and glared at me. "Why are you being such a pain?"

"Why? How about I almost got killed yesterday. Hanging out with me isn't a great idea." I glanced at my watch. "Look, it's late. I gotta go." I got up from the table and put my bowl in the sink. "This is the only chance I'll get to talk to Harrison Smith. If I miss him now . . ."

"Yeah? Then what?" she said.

I sighed. "Admit it. We're at a dead end. There's a chance—okay, it's a small chance—that Harrison found some connection between Powell and Sneider. Harrison said it himself—all we need is reasonable doubt to prove that Dave is innocent."

"I get that. But I told you before that I'm in this to the end."

"No. Okay?" I leaned up against the sink and stared at her. Why was she making this so difficult? It wasn't like I wanted to go alone. Everything was easier when I was with Rusty. She knew what I was thinking before I did. But I couldn't handle it if something happened to her.

Rusty shot me a frosty look. She wasn't happy. "Fine," she muttered. She shoved her chair back and started clearing the table. "You go your way, I'll go mine."

"What are you talking about? Go where?"

She ignored me. She shoved the cereal box in the cabinet and slammed the door shut. Did she think I'd back down and let her come with me?

I checked my backpack for the millionth time. The

photograph and Sneider's note were in the front zip pocket. "So we'll talk later?" I tried to sound upbeat, like everything was okay. I slipped my backpack on.

She wasn't falling for it. "Yeah . . . later." She breezed past me. She grabbed her jacket and stormed out the front door.

"Where are you going?" I called out after her. I ran out the door behind her. "Rusty, what are you doing?" She ignored me, grabbed her bike from the front porch, and pedaled down the drive.

I hopped on my bike too. I thought about racing after her. I even thought about telling her she could come along with me.

But I didn't.

At the end of the drive she took a left. I hesitated for a second, then hung a right toward town and my meeting with Harrison Smith. I didn't have a choice, did I? Miss it and that was it. He'd be on his way to DC later today, so this was my only chance to talk to him. I told myself I was making the right decision. I only hoped I was right.

CHAPTER XLIV

Harrison's office was on the second floor of a two-story building on Washington. A central corridor ran through the floor with lots of beige walls and carpets, a FedEx box, and some plastic plants to make it feel like home. On either side of the hallway were office suites. I walked past five of them before I reached his office at the end of the hallway. It was the only one with a light on, so it wasn't hard to spot. I tapped on the door.

It swung open immediately. "Oz, good morning," Harrison said. I looked past him. The rest of the office was dark. It looked like it was just us. He grabbed his jacket from a coatrack and slipped it on. "I'm sorry to do this but I have to cancel our meeting."

"But—I—"

"Something's come up." He flicked off the office light and closed the door behind him.

"But—but you said—," I stammered.

"I know," he said, interrupting me. "Trust me. I wouldn't do this if it weren't urgent." He brushed past me and walked quickly down the hallway. He paused at the elevator, then changed his mind and headed for the stairs.

"It will only take a few minutes. I brought the photograph." I patted my backpack. "It's right here."

I caught up with him at the top of the stairwell.

"Please," I said. I couldn't believe I was begging this guy, but I didn't care. I had to find out if A. J. Powell was Sapphire.

Harrison looked at me but didn't say anything. His brow was furrowed and his jaw was set. Something was wrong.

"What? What is it?" I asked.

"Oz, I'm not going to lie to you." He let out a long sigh and said, "Just before you got here the police called. There is a situation. . . ."

"*Situation?* What kind of situation?"

He started down the stairs. I raced after him.

"Is it something to do with Sneider's murder?"

He didn't answer.

"It is, isn't it?" I said. I jumped down the last two steps. "Tell me . . . what's going on?"

"The call I got from the police . . . they're at A. J. Powell's house."

"What?" My head spun. "How . . . ?" Suddenly it was clear. "This *does* have something to do with the murder, doesn't it?"

"I'm afraid it does." He adjusted his left shirtsleeve and twirled his cuff link as he thought for a moment. "From what they said, it sounds like they've got some evidence that links Powell to Sneider's murder."

"What? You're kidding. Do you mean . . . ?"

He nodded. "Yes. They think Powell killed Sneider."

A massive weight lifted off my shoulders. "But that's great—that's . . ." I couldn't believe it. If the police had fingered Powell, then . . .

Harrison shook his head. His face was grim. All hard lines. "Walk with me to my car. I'll tell you what I know." He crossed the courtyard toward the street. I followed close on his heels.

"Apparently Powell has barricaded himself in his house," he continued. "He says the entire place is wired—explosives, trip wires, the works. Alcohol, Tobacco, and Firearms are on their way. So is the FBI." He looked over at me. "He's threatening to blow himself up along with a hostage—a young girl."

I did a double take. "A . . . young girl?"

"No positive ID yet, but they should have more info soon."

My mind reeled. Rusty? Was *she* the hostage? Was that where she'd gone this morning—to Powell's house? Then what? The police showed up? Powell panicked and grabbed her as a hostage?

But she wouldn't have gone to Powell's on her own, would she? Then I remembered how angry she'd been when I told her she couldn't come with me. *You go your way, I'll go mine.* I'd never seen her so mad before. She could have done anything. . . .

"The police asked for my help." Harrison's voice broke through my thoughts. "Since A. J. and I worked together, they're hoping I can talk some sense into him . . . convince him to release the girl and turn himself in."

My head snapped up. "You worked with Powell?" I replayed our phone call last night. When I'd asked Harrison if he knew Powell, he'd sounded vague.

"I was his boss."

I felt like I'd had the wind knocked out of me. I couldn't believe what he was saying.

He smiled apologetically. "I didn't tell you because I wasn't sure what you were up to. That's why I wanted to meet." He pulled his keys out of his jacket pocket and pressed the unlock button on the key chain. Car lights flashed on his Lexus. Aside from his car, the street was empty.

"I know this is a lot to throw at you. We'll meet as soon as it's over. I promise. I'll let you know what happens." He walked over to the driver's side and opened the door.

"I'm going with you."

"Out of the question."

"You don't understand," I blurted out. "He's got Rusty."

Harrison was about to climb into the car, but that stopped him. He spun around. "Rusty? Who's Rusty?"

"My friend. I think she might be the one he's holding hostage."

My voice broke. Just saying the words made me feel sick . . . the thought of Powell holding her hostage . . . Why hadn't I listened to her? Why hadn't I let her come with me? Then none of this would have happened.

"We met Powell," I stammered. "Rusty and me. At his house."

"You what?" he barked.

"I can't explain now. But I think she might have gone

back there. So I'm going. Either I go with you or I go on my own."

I watched his face. He was trying to figure out what to do. He rubbed his forehead and looked over at me.

"Put your bike in here," he said, popping the trunk.

His voice was stern, angry even, but it didn't matter. I jogged over and unlocked my bike where I'd chained it up. I quickly ran back to the car.

I threw my bike into the trunk and slammed it shut. I rushed over to the passenger seat and jumped in before he could change his mind.

Harrison pulled the car out of the parking space. "Listen to me very carefully. Do exactly what I say. If I say stay back, you stay back. If I tell you to wait in the car, you wait." He glanced over at me. His face was steely and his blue eyes were hard. "Am I clear?"

I nodded.

"This isn't a game. I don't know what you've been up to, but I'll get to the bottom of it, I promise. So you'd better start at the beginning. . . ."

CHAPTER XLV

I told Harrison everything on the way to Powell's place. He asked a few questions, but mostly he listened.

"I think Sneider figured out my dad wasn't a spy," I said. "He came to Santa Fe to find out the identity of Sapphire—his source—and why he'd made up the story about my dad."

"But how did Sneider figure out Powell was Sapphire?" Harrison interrupted. "Sapphire was an anonymous source, wasn't he?"

"Yeah, but we found a photo in Sneider's motel room." Harrison shot me a look. I kept talking so he couldn't hassle me about breaking into Sneider's room. "It was a picture of three men: my dad, a man named Victor Martinez, and A. J. Powell. On the back of the photo,

Sneider had written 'Sapphire.' He must have figured out that either Powell or Martinez was Sapphire. Martinez is dead—probably murdered."

"So that left Powell?" Harrison said.

"Yeah. Powell set up a fake meeting between Sneider and my brother to frame Dave. He killed Sneider and left the body at Chez Isabelle."

I glanced up. We were at Powell's place. Harrison pulled over next to the Calle Cabrillo street sign and cut the engine. I couldn't believe Rusty and I had been here just a few days ago. So much had happened since then. And now this . . . I tried to be positive, but I had a bad feeling about Rusty. Why had I let her go off on her own? If something happened to her, it was all my fault.

I craned my neck and looked around. We were too far away to see Powell's house, but it was quiet and the place looked deserted.

"Where is everybody?" I said. "I don't see the police."

Harrison's jaw was set, and he looked tense. He lowered his voice. "Apparently there's an access road that leads to the back of Powell's place. That's where the SWAT team is positioned. I'm meeting the hostage negotiator over there," he said, pointing to the path that led to Powell's house. "I'll see if I can talk some sense into A. J." He unbuckled his seat belt and swiveled around to face me. "I'll find out what's going on. Stay here. I'll be back as soon as I can."

I nodded, then pulled out my cell. I started to punch in Rusty's number. Harrison leaned over and grabbed my arm. "Switch it off. *No phones.*"

I hit the end button. "I only wanted to see if I could get Rusty."

"You'll know soon enough if she's in there. In the meantime, if her phone starts ringing, it could push Powell over the edge."

He was right. I switched it off, then watched as he got out, closed the door, and headed up the road. I lost sight of him at the turnoff to the house. I drummed my fingers on the dashboard. I checked my watch. He'd been gone only a minute, but it felt like forever.

I stopped drumming. I'd forgotten to tell Harrison about Powell's dog, Rio. What if Rio attacked Harrison like he'd attacked Rusty? I jumped out of the car. I had to warn him. I listened but couldn't hear anything. No barking. Where was the dog? Something was wrong.

A single gunshot shattered the silence. A second shot followed. I sprinted toward the house. I'd promised to stay in the car, but too bad. Powell had Rusty, I was sure of it. I had to get her out of there. Loud barking pierced the air. It was Powell's dog. I picked up speed. Rounded the corner. The front yard was straight ahead, the house in the distance. The metal gate was swinging open. I ran into the yard. I spun around madly.

The first thing I saw was Rio. He was tied to a metal stake driven into the ground on my left. He was snarling and barking like crazy. He yanked desperately at the stake. What was it? My eyes followed his. I took a step toward the house. My heart skipped a beat. I took another step, then stopped. It was Powell. He was on the porch, slumped in a metal chair. Blood was everywhere. He wasn't moving. Dead.

My eyes darted across the porch.

"Rusty!" I yelled. Where was she? And where were Harrison and the police? Why weren't they doing anything?

"She's not here."

I spun around, startled to find Harrison Smith standing next to me.

"Just you and me."

My eyes moved swiftly from the house to Harrison. His face was cold, but there was the glimmer of a smile on his lips. He didn't say a word. But then again, he didn't have to. The gun he pointed at me said everything.

CHAPTER XLVI

Harrison Smith adjusted the black leather gloves he was wearing. His shirt cuff slipped out from his jacket sleeve, and that's when I saw it: a silver cuff link with a blue stone set in the center. I glanced from the cuff link to his face.

"You're Sapphire, aren't you?" I blurted out. He caught my eye and gazed briefly at the cuff link. He raised his eyebrows and gave me a half smile.

"The sapphire cuff links? My signature." He waved the gun at me. "Walk, please."

I did what he said. I forced myself to look straight ahead. *Don't look at Powell.* I knew if I did, I'd lose it. I couldn't afford that. Harrison pressed the gun into my back, a reminder to keep walking.

"It's easy to fake a suicide," he said, as if reading my mind. His voice was flat, matter-of-fact, like he was discussing the weather. "If the person trusts you, it makes the element of surprise that much greater. Stop right there," Harrison commanded.

We were about thirty feet from the house. I scoped out the yard quickly. Powell's dog was directly to my left. He was yanking at the stake so hard that his collar choked him. *He's trying to get to Powell*, I thought.

I shivered. Don't lose it. Focus. Think about Rusty.

"Turn and face me," Harrison said.

I did what he said. My back was to the house now. I stared straight at him.

"Where's Rusty?" I demanded. "What did you do to her?"

"Nothing. I had to make sure you joined me." Harrison smiled his thin half smile. "She was the bait."

I shuddered, remembering how I'd begged to come along. I'd been so stupid. I'd played right into his hands.

He smiled. "Don't beat yourself up. I knew you'd do anything to save your friend." He shook his head. "You've become quite a problem, Oz. So persistent. I hoped you'd lose interest, but you wouldn't let it drop, would you? When you called yesterday, I knew I had to do something.

I had unfinished business with Powell. So I decided to—excuse the expression—kill two birds with one stone."

Rio let out a long, low growl. I glanced over at him. He was lying on the ground but alert, his eyes fixed on Powell.

I looked back at Harrison. "It won't work. The police will figure out what happened. They'll see—"

"See *what*?" Harrison interrupted. "Oz, look around. No neighbors. No passing cars. And it's not like A. J. got any visitors."

"But the gunshots," I said.

"If anyone did hear them, they'll figure it was just some innocent target practice." He smiled. "Besides, I won't be here long."

He was right. I was alone. No one was going to help me.

"If you *are* found," he continued, "there is a perfectly reasonable explanation. You came here to confront A. J. You accused him of betraying your father. He pulled a gun on you. You ran. He shot you in the back. Realizing what he'd done, that the game was up, he shot himself."

"The police will find out I visited your office. Rusty will tell them. They'll know you're involved."

"No offense, Oz, but you're not worth their time. I'll take that photo you kindly brought with you, so there's no evidence linking me to Sneider's murder. If they do ask,

I'll say you stopped by my office. You were hysterical." He shrugged. "Maybe you were on drugs. Who are they going to believe? A dead teenager or an upstanding citizen and soon-to-be U.S. senator?"

"That's what this is all about, isn't it?" I said, clenching my fists. "It's all about your Senate campaign?"

The smile faded from Harrison Smith's lips. His eyes were icy.

"I didn't want any of this to happen. I had no choice. You were warned, but you didn't listen." He made it sound like it was my fault. I thought about the car running me off the road. The break-in at my home . . . all messages to back off.

"But what about my dad? Why frame him?"

Harrison shook his head. "Don't be naive. Your dad wasn't an innocent victim. He was part of it."

His words hit me like a slap. "You're lying."

"I recruited your dad. He wanted the money, pure and simple."

There was a crushing pain in my chest. My hands flew up to my ears. "No, I don't believe it. It's not true."

"Your mom was pregnant with you. Another mouth to feed. He did the math and figured my offer was a good one."

Hot tears burned my eyes. I choked them back. "No, no, no," I murmured.

"The only problem was that he got cold feet. He lost it and told me he couldn't go through with it. But it was too late. How could I trust him to keep his mouth shut?"

I looked up. "So you . . . ?"

Harrison jumped in. "So I planted documents on him. That way if he ever decided to talk, no one would believe him."

"But why? Why do it?"

Harrison looked at me like I was the dumb kid in class. "Money, Oz. People, governments, dictators—are all willing to pay top dollar for nuclear weapons secrets. They wanted what I had. I wanted their money. With their money I could buy power—"

"Like a U.S. Senate seat?"

"Clever boy," he said, smiling. "Campaigns aren't cheap."

My brain swirled. "But Sneider . . . how did he figure into it?"

"I needed someone outside to break the story and point the finger at your dad. It was a brilliant move. I chose an obscure journalist from an obscure scientific journal. I knew he wouldn't ask too many questions. He was too desperate for his big break."

"My dad . . . did you . . ." I wasn't sure I could get the words out, but I had to. "Did you kill him, too?"

"The heart attack?" He shook his head. "I can't take credit for that, I'm afraid. Just a bum ticker."

"And Victor Martinez?"

Harrison scowled. "Victor was a problem. He was convinced your father was innocent. I asked Powell to take care of it. Looking back, it was a mistake. Powell wasn't cut out for the job. Nearly botched it, and afterward he demanded more money to keep his mouth shut."

My brain raced as I tried to take in everything he'd told me. "And Mrs. Martinez?"

Harrison smiled. "She's been the recipient of anonymous 'donations' ever since her husband died."

"So she'd back off?"

Harrison shrugged. "Something like that."

"But why kill Aaron Sneider after all this time?"

Harrison's brow furrowed. "Sneider decided to write a book. He started digging around. He asked too many questions . . . wanted to find out who Sapphire was. That was the last straw."

"So you set up a fake meeting with Dave so you could kill Sneider?"

Harrison shook his head again. "You watch too much

television, Oz. It wasn't that bloodthirsty. The idea was to scare Sneider off. Remind him that if the story came out, his whole career was over. But he was stubborn. He refused. Things got out of hand and . . ." He shrugged.

"But why blame Dave? Why pin Sneider's death on my family?"

"Because"—he smiled again—"it was easy. Your brother made the perfect suspect—means, motive, and opportunity, as they say. But cheer up. Your brother may well be exonerated. Your friend Rusty will tell the police you thought Powell was the killer. They'll figure you came here to confront him. Your brother will be freed. That is what you wanted, wasn't it?"

His words cut through me. He was right. Dave would be free. I'd gotten what I wanted. But not like this. There had to be a way out.

"And the photograph?" I added quickly. "The one of my dad, Powell, and Martinez?"

"Ah yes . . . the infamous photograph . . ."

"Sneider wrote 'Sapphire' on the back of it. But you're not in the picture."

Harrison laughed. "No, I'm not. But I *took* the photograph and sent it to Sneider to use in his article."

I squeezed my eyes shut. It suddenly made sense. All

along we'd assumed Sneider meant that one of the men in the photo was Sapphire. We'd gotten it wrong. Really wrong.

But something was bothering me. Powell. Sneider. The murder. I couldn't put my finger on it. What was it?

"But—," I said.

"Enough," interrupted Harrison. "Time is up."

He walked toward me. I knew what he was going to do. He'd walk up to the house and shoot me in the back. He'd kill me, and no one would ever know what happened. I quickly scanned the gate at the edge of Powell's property. Could I make a run for it? Harrison stopped next to me. He leaned so close that I felt his breath on my face.

"You're thinking about running, aren't you? You're wondering how quickly you can get out of this yard and into those trees."

I gulped but didn't move.

"I wouldn't recommend it. You won't make it. This gun"—he pressed the barrel into my temple—"is small but surprisingly powerful. And I'm a good shot. If you try to run, I'll kill you. But very slowly. Either way you die, but this way will be much less painful, I promise."

Harrison walked toward the house. As soon as he took a step, Powell's dog leaped up. He went ballistic. The metal stake moved slightly. The closer Harrison got to the house, the more mental Rio became. My heart raced. If Rio were loose, he'd attack Harrison, I knew he would. I stole a look at the stake. But was he powerful enough to pull the stake out of the ground?

Harrison's shoes hit the first porch step. Rio hurled himself toward him. The stake moved again. Another step. A little bit more. But not enough. I needed more time.

The footsteps stopped. Was Harrison on the porch now? Aiming his gun at my back? What did I have—a few seconds? I took a deep breath. I had one chance. That was it.

I stared at Powell's dog.

I willed him to listen to me.

Then I shouted as loudly as I could:

"ATAQUE!"

CHAPTER XLVII

"ATAQUE!"

It was the command Powell had used. As soon as he heard it, the dog lunged toward the house, ripping the stake out of the ground. It trailed behind him. He was a blur of fur and snarling teeth.

Harrison saw what was happening. But he was too late. He swiveled and aimed the gun at the dog. Rio was already up the stairs. The dog leaped, slamming into Harrison's chest and throwing him to the ground. Harrison let out a bloodcurdling scream. The gun flew from his hand and spun across the porch.

I watched it happen like it was in slow motion. Powell's dog was about to kill Harrison. Part of me didn't care. *Go ahead. Kill him.* He was going to kill me, wasn't he? How could I stop him anyway?

Blood pounded in my ears. I couldn't breathe. Then I saw Powell's dead body. I had to do something. I tried to suck in some air. If I let Rio kill Harrison, then I was a murderer too, right?

I took another breath, deeper this time. I wasn't sure it would work.

"*Basta!*" I called.

My voice cracked. It was the command Powell had used to call his dog off Rusty. But I wasn't even sure he'd heard me.

"*BASTA!*"

My voice was steadier this time. The dog's head snapped up. He looked confused. He still had Harrison pinned to the ground. I walked slowly toward him, trying not to let him see that I was shaking.

"*BASTA.*"

Reluctantly Rio released Harrison. Harrison moaned and curled up into a ball.

The dog looked at me, then at Powell.

"It's okay, boy," I said. He whimpered and trotted over to Powell's side. He shoved his nose at Powell's hand like he was trying to wake him up. I ran up the steps and knelt down beside Harrison. He was okay, but it looked like he was in shock. I loosened his collar and tie. His skin was cold and clammy.

I glanced over at Rio. He could change his mind at any minute and go after Harrison or me. I wasn't going to wait to find out. I stood up and grabbed Harrison under his arms. I hoisted him up. He must have weighed 180 pounds and right now, it was all dead weight. I struggled to drag him across the porch. All the time I kept an eye on the dog.

I propped Harrison up against the wall and opened the screen door. Sweat poured down my back and face. It was only a couple of yards, but I was out of breath. I wiped my face on my shirt. I pulled Harrison over the threshold and into the house. It took a second for my eyes to adjust to the darkness. The curtains were drawn, and it smelled like stale cigarette smoke.

I laid Harrison on the floor and grabbed a grubby quilt from the sofa. I draped it around him.

I scanned the room quickly, but I couldn't see the phone Powell had used the other day. I thought about hunting for it but figured it would be quicker to get mine from Harrison's car. I ran back out into the sunshine and squinted over at Powell and the dog. Rio was lying down next to him with his head resting on Powell's foot. I kicked Harrison's gun off the porch. It landed in a clump of weeds, hidden.

I darted across the yard and back to the car. My phone was on the seat where I'd left it. I turned it back on. I grabbed my backpack and fumbled inside until I found Detective Suarez's card. My hands were shaking, but I managed to punch in the numbers. He picked up on the first ring. When I heard his voice, something snapped. I lost it. It was hearing a voice—a real, live voice—that did it. Suddenly everything that had happened hit me like a ton of bricks. I don't know how he figured out what I was trying to say, but he did.

"Stay where you are. We'll be there in five minutes," he said.

I made a second call. Rusty didn't pick up. It went straight to her voice mail.

"Rusty, call me." I paused for a second. I wanted to say something more, but I couldn't find the words. "Just call me." I hung up and stared at the phone, trying to figure out what to do. I had to find her. I had to know she was okay. I tried her home number. No answer. School. I checked my watch. It was between periods. I hit speed dial and called our friend Zach.

"Zach? It's Oz. Have you seen Rusty?"

"Where are you, man?"

"I'll explain later. I'm trying to find Rusty." My teeth were chattering. I clenched my jaws tight until they stopped, then said, "Have you seen her?"

"She didn't show up this morning. I figured she was with you," he said.

"No . . . no . . . she's not with me. Listen, if you see her, tell her to call me?"

"Sure. No worries."

I hit end. There was a hole in the bottom of my stomach. Where was she? I had to talk to her.

I played back what Harrison had said. He'd said he hadn't hurt Rusty. The question was, could I believe him?

CHAPTER XLVIII

Suarez was right about one thing: In minutes Powell's place was crawling with cops, ambulances, CSIs, the works. I kept thinking that Rusty would have loved it. All this cop stuff was her thing. Only problem was she wasn't here, and I didn't know where she was. My stomach had that sick feeling. I looked at my cell for the millionth time. No texts. No messages from her. Nothing. I'd called Zach at school again, but she wasn't there, either.

"I spoke to Archie McCallister and he asked us to drop you off at his home."

I'd been so busy thinking about Rusty that I hadn't even heard Suarez walk up. I shook my head, trying to clear it.

"I'm sorry, what did you say?"

"We're going to drop you off at Archie McCallister's place, just as soon as we're done."

Archie? Something snapped in my brain. Harrison was paying off Linda Martinez to keep her quiet, right? Archie knew Linda too. He'd been at her place at least twice, according to Linda's neighbor. A coincidence? I thought back to meeting Harrison outside Archie's office . . . how Archie had asked Harrison to give me a ride. Another coincidence? Were Harrison and Archie in on this together?

"Oz, are you sure you're all right? I know the paramedics gave you the okay, but I'd still like to get you checked out at the hospital."

"Yes, I'm okay. Really." But I wasn't. There was no way I was going to Archie's house, no matter what Suarez said. Suarez gave me a weird look.

"It's Rusty," I said. "I still can't get ahold of her."

"Oz, I'm sure she's fine."

"But what if Harrison . . ."

Suarez held up his hand to stop me.

"Oz, you told me yourself that Harrison said he hadn't touched Rusty. And why would he? He was counting on her to finger Powell. It was part of his plan. He had everything he wanted from you—the note and the photograph. With you dead, she wasn't a threat."

When he said it like that, I almost believed him. He made it sound so logical. But still . . . I couldn't get rid of this feeling that something was wrong.

"Besides," he continued, "the most important thing you can do right now is to help us here. I want you to tell me exactly what happened one more time. We'll do a formal statement later, but we need to go over everything now while it's fresh."

"But I've told you what happened." It was true. I'd told him everything. When I told him we had broken into Sneider's motel room, he'd given me a "We'll talk about that later" look, but to be honest, he'd been pretty cool about everything.

"You're upset. I understand," he continued. "You've been through a lot. I promise we'll get you out of here as soon as possible." That was cop talk for not anytime soon. "Why don't you grab a bottle of water from the guys? I'll be with you in a minute."

I nodded okay, but it wasn't okay.

I walked toward the police car. A couple of cops looked over at me but didn't say anything. I kept walking. Act like you know what you're doing and no one hassles you.

When I reached Harrison's car, there were some CSIs working it over. I stole a glance at my bike in the open trunk. I looked at the CSIs. There was no way I'd get it out without them seeing me.

I walked quietly past them. If they asked, I'd say I was stretching my legs. But they didn't say anything. They were too busy to notice. When I hit the corner I took a left onto El Rancho. When I was sure no one could see me, I started to jog. Then I started to run. Ten minutes and I'd be at West Alameda. Then . . . then what? I'd look for Rusty.

It was the only way. Suarez had his priorities. I had mine. And if he wasn't going to find Rusty, then I was.

CHAPTER XLIX

Rusty's house was empty. No sign of her or her parents. I wasn't surprised. I'd called her cell and home number enough times to know they weren't here. The truth was, I couldn't think of anywhere else to go. And deep down I hoped I was wrong. I'd find them all here. Safe. Nice dream.

I did a quick loop around the first floor. I was running on fumes, but I had to keep moving. I could crash once I'd found Rusty. I poked my head in the kitchen. My cereal bowl was in the sink where I'd left it earlier that morning. I stopped and stared at it for a second. Everything looked so . . . normal. But nothing was normal anymore, was it?

I shook my head. *Focus. Find Rusty.* I glanced out the

window and down the drive. Where had she gone this morning? If there was a clue, it had to be in her bedroom. I ran upstairs. My eyes raced around her room looking for something, anything that could tell me where she was.

My cell rang. I fished it out of my pocket. It was Suarez. I hesitated. I almost hit reject. But what if he'd found Rusty? I answered it.

"Have you found her?"

"What do you think you're doing?" Suarez barked, ignoring my question. He was mad. Ticked off. I should have been freaked out—he was a cop, right? But today was different. I'd seen my second dead body, and someone had tried to kill me. Suarez didn't scare me as much anymore.

"I told you. I've got to find Rusty."

I rooted around in Rusty's desk, looking for a clue that would tell me where she'd gone.

Suarez growled. He spoke slowly so I wouldn't miss the message. "Oz, you're the witness to a murder. You left a crime scene, which is against the law. Not to mention breaking and entering, and tampering with evidence. It's a long list. So don't mess with me. Tell me where you are *now*."

Everything was in neat piles on Rusty's desk. Very Rusty. On top of a folder I found a new yellow legal pad.

"Did you hear what I said? Where are you? Oz, if you

don't tell me, I'll trace your cell phone. Don't make me waste my time," he snapped.

I was about to toss the legal pad aside but stopped.

The page was blank except for one sentence written in neat block handwriting.

CSI RULE #1: GO BACK TO THE SCENE OF THE CRIME!!!

I ran my finger over the words. *Scene of the crime?* What did she mean? Was she talking about Sneider's murder? If she was, then what? Did she mean Chez Isabelle? Is that where she was?

"Oz . . . ?"

"I'm at Rusty's," I blurted out.

I didn't mind telling Suarez where I was. It was no big deal. I'd be gone before he got here. I left my cell phone on Rusty's desk. If Suarez tried to track it, he wouldn't get very far. By the time he figured out what was going on, I'd be at Chez Isabelle.

CHAPTER L

I grabbed a bike from the shed in Rusty's backyard. The seat was too low, but I didn't bother adjusting it. All I wanted was to get to Chez Isabelle and find Rusty. I still had the adrenaline rush from this morning. I didn't feel tired, just wired and jittery.

On the way over, I kept telling myself everything was okay. The cops had Harrison. He'd killed Sneider and Powell. Dave was clear and Chez Isabelle could open again. Good news, right? And Rusty? She was probably at Chez Isabelle right now, snooping around for clues. She knew we kept a key under the rosemary plant by the back door. . . .

A thought struck me. How had Harrison and Powell

gotten into Chez Isabelle? The door was unlocked when I got there Saturday morning. The lock wasn't broken. Did they know we kept a spare key? Or maybe Powell picked the lock? I tried to imagine what had happened Friday night. They must have waited until Dave left, then . . . then what?

I wasn't thinking clearly. There was too much junk in my head right now. *Find Rusty*, I thought. *She'll be able to figure it out.*

I hit the parking lot. I'd made it there in record time. The lot was empty except for a car. It was Razor's. Probably stopping by to make sure everything was okay. I leaned the bike against the wall and raced over to the back door. My heart was beating faster. I couldn't wait to tell him what had happened. He'd never believe it. I yanked open the door.

"Razor?"

There he was, to the left by the sinks. He was getting something from the first aid cabinet. His back was to me, but he spun around as soon as he heard my voice.

"Oz . . . ?" His face was white as a sheet. There was something in his hand. Small, flat, plastic. His fingers snapped shut over it before I could see what it was.

"I didn't mean to scare you," I said. "Are you okay? Did

you cut yourself?" I motioned toward the first aid cabinet.

Razor didn't answer. His eyes darted back and forth.

"Razor? What's wrong?"

Razor shook his head like he was trying to clear it. "Nothing. I just wasn't expecting to see anybody. You by yourself?" He closed the cabinet quickly.

"Yeah. Actually, I'm looking for Rusty. Have you seen her?"

"Rusty?"

"Yeah. I kind of thought she'd be here."

"Why? What's going on?" Razor asked, clearing his throat.

"Sorry." I smiled. "I'm not making any sense." I reached for my cell phone, then remembered I'd left it at Rusty's. I'd call her on the office phone. "Look, I gotta call Rusty, then I'll tell you everything. Maybe she'll finally pick up this time. Back in two secs." I started toward the office, but Razor caught my arm.

"Whoa. Slow down. You can call her in a minute. What's happening?"

"Sorry. I'm all over the place." He was right. I'd already left Rusty a million messages. I took a deep breath, then said, "I figured out who killed Sneider."

Razor went bug-eyed. "What? Who?"

I laughed. "I know, I know—can you believe it? You remember that guy who eats here all the time? Harrison Smith? He did it. Well, he and another guy . . ." I almost said *Powell* but stopped. Even now, after everything that had happened, something didn't feel right. Powell was a mess when Rusty and I saw him. I had a hard time imagining him holding Sneider down, let alone stabbing him. Still . . .

"Oz? Did you hear what I said? Where's this guy Harrison now?"

"The police have him." I looked over at Razor. No ripped T-shirts today. He was wearing a white linen shirt, a black belt with a silver buckle, and black jeans. "What's up? You got a hot date tonight?"

Razor frowned. "I was going to leave a note."

"What are you talking about?"

"Actually, I'm on my way to the airport," he said.

"Airport . . . ?"

"I got a job offer. In New York City. I just found out, and they need me to start immediately."

I felt my chest tighten. He had to be kidding. "You can't. Razor, don't you get it? It's all over. They've got the guy who did it. Dave will be out of jail today. Mom's on her way back. We'll be open for business tomorrow."

Razor shook his head. "Oz, it's too late. I already said yes. It's an incredible opportunity. Head chef at a great place. I can't say no. Chez Isabelle will be fine without me." He gave me a smile and turned to go.

"That's it? You're leaving just like that?"

He ignored me and headed toward the door.

All the anger and fear I'd felt in the last couple of days surged up inside me. It was like a big adrenaline bubble that had to burst. Before I knew what I was doing, I'd reached out and grabbed Razor's arm. I had to stop him.

I must have caught him off balance. He swung around and grabbed the prep table to steady himself. Whatever he'd been holding flew out of his hand and hit the ground.

It skidded across the floor until it hit the base of the walk-in. It stopped. I stared at it blankly. A computer memory stick . . . ? Razor had a memory stick in the first aid cabinet? Why? Our eyes met. It must have been something really important. Razor's eyes narrowed slightly. My stomach clenched. Something was wrong.

Get out, shouted a voice inside me. I lunged for the door. Too late. Razor slammed into me, steamrolling me into the counter. The wind was knocked out of me. I doubled over, clutching my sides, gasping for breath. He grabbed something. I tried to straighten up. He was holding something shiny, metal. His hand was at my throat. He pressed the edge of a chef's knife against my neck like I was a piece of meat he was about to butcher.

"Bad timing, Oz. Really bad timing."

I looked at his face. He wasn't smiling anymore. Neither was I.

CHAPTER LI

He held the knife with one hand. With the other, he yanked a box of plastic wrap across the counter.

"On the ground," Razor said, pushing me down. I fell to my knees. He gave me another shove. I landed flat on my face. "Hands behind your back."

My heart was pounding. Sweat broke out on my forehead. *This isn't happening*, I thought. *Razor's my friend, he's* . . .

Razor's voice broke through my thoughts. "Don't move." His voice was calm, like he was about to show me how to clarify stock or julienne a carrot. It was surreal, like nothing was wrong.

"Razor," I choked. "What's going on? I don't get it."

"You're not supposed to be here," he said matter-of-factly, as he tugged at the plastic wrap. "Which means Harrison screwed up."

Harrison had an accomplice. Someone strong enough to hold Sneider down. Someone powerful enough to knife him. Someone with a key to Chez Isabelle. It wasn't Powell.

"You were Harrison's accomplice, weren't you?" I said, craning my neck, trying to see his face. He was twirling the plastic into a long coil. He wrapped it tightly around my wrists.

Razor ignored me. "There. That should do it." He gave my wrists a pat, like he was admiring his handiwork. It was so tight, I could feel my hands going numb. He yanked me up by the elbows. Pain shot through my shoulders. He pulled me to my feet.

He turned me around so I faced him. I searched his face, looking for the old Razor. But he was gone. Panic rushed through me. *He's going to kill me. I'm going to die.*

Like he knew what I was thinking, he said gently, "Oz, I'm not going to hurt you. Just do what I say, okay?" My throat wouldn't work. I couldn't say anything. He repeated himself. "I said, *okay?*" This time his voice was louder, more insistent.

I swallowed. I moved my head up and down slowly. "That's better."

"Why?" I finally said. "Harrison and you . . . I don't get it."

Razor swept a hand through his hair and thought for a minute. "I owed him. He helped me out back in DC."

"I don't get it."

"I was dealing, okay?" I just stared at him. He shook his head. "Oz, don't look at me like that. It was no biggie. Only I had a problem with a client. Things got bad and I knifed him. I didn't mean to, but that didn't really matter. I could have done some serious time."

"So Harrison helped you out?"

"He was a regular at the restaurant. I called him in a panic. He said he'd take care of it, and he did."

"And Sneider . . . ?"

"That was payback. Harrison told me some old reporter was snooping around in Santa Fe. He was worried he'd show up at Chez Isabelle, so he asked me to keep an eye out for him. Friday night Sneider showed up. I'm making the rounds, chatting up the tables like I do. I stop by his table and make small talk. Then he asks me to give a note to Dave."

"To set up a meeting, right?"

"Yep. I called Harrison. He freaked and said there was no way I could let this guy meet Dave. But I knew Sneider wasn't going to give up. He had that look. I figured, why not set up a meeting, only he meets me, not Dave? I talk some sense into him. Explain that he needs to back off. So I went back to his table and told him Dave would meet him here after closing."

"Only it didn't work out that way, did it?"

Razor gave me a half smile. "No. Dave said he'd close, but that was cool. I'd told Sneider to come back at midnight. I knew Dave would be gone by then. I went to El Farol after work as usual, then headed back to Chez Isabelle."

"You broke the back door light, didn't you?" I said.

"Good eye, Oz." Razor smiled weakly.

"So then what happened?"

"Sneider went nuts when he found out Dave wasn't here. Accused me of lying. Started to storm off. Said he knew where you lived and that he was going there to talk to Dave." Razor shook his head slowly. "I couldn't let that happen."

"So you killed him?" My voice was only a whisper.

Razor frowned. "It wasn't like that. I grabbed him. I wanted to knock some sense into him. I shoved him against the wall. Then he decides to fight back." Razor shook his head. "Idiot. I hit him again but harder this time. He slipped . . . must have knocked his head. Next thing I know, he's on the floor. I look down and he's out. The guy is barely breathing, and I've got a big problem."

"Why didn't you call an ambulance? Get some help?"

Razor rolled his eyes. "Grow up, Oz. With my record? No." He shook his head. "I didn't have a choice, did I? I called Harrison. Told him things hadn't gone according to plan and to get his butt over here."

"That was when you stabbed Sneider, wasn't it?"

"I told you, Oz. I didn't have a choice."

"But you knew the cops would think Dave did it. He's your friend. How could you do that?"

Razor laughed. "Friends? Me and Dave? I don't think so. When I came back from DC, he never stopped reminding me how much better he was than me. He made sure I never forgot what a big favor he was doing by hiring me." He scowled. "I hated it. Pinning this on Dave was the only good thing that came out of it."

Everything was falling apart. I couldn't breathe. Razor had killed Sneider, right here, at Chez Isabelle. I tried to make it clear in my mind, but I couldn't. Sneider's murder was just the start, wasn't it? Razor set Dave up.

And me . . . ? He knew Harrison was going to kill me, didn't he? And he didn't care. I didn't matter.

I tried to push those thoughts away. I had to keep going. Keep Razor talking. "The memory stick," I mumbled. "Is that what was on Sneider's computer?"

"My insurance policy," he said. "I told Harrison I'd trashed Sneider's computer. I didn't tell him I'd copied the files."

"So you hid the memory stick in the first aid cabinet."

"Tuesday, when we reopened. It was the perfect spot, since the police had already searched the place." He straightened up. Suddenly he was all business. "So here's the deal. I need you to disappear for a bit. Just for a while, until things blow over."

He touched my shoulder. "Don't worry. We'll go for a drive." I froze. "You'll ride in the trunk. I'll drop you off somewhere safe, I promise."

He was smiling, but his eyes were dark and cold. He was lying. He was going to kill me. Plain and simple.

"You don't have to do that, Razor. I won't tell anyone. I promise." Now we were both lying.

"I know you wouldn't. But my plan's better. Trust me." He stuck the tip of the knife into my back. "Let's go."

I took a step. My mind raced, trying to figure a way

out. If I got in the trunk, I was dead. Too many ways to disappear. Send the car off a cliff into a canyon. Torch the car with me in it. Lots of ways to kill me, and no one would ever know.

I took another step. Not much time. I had to run. I'd wait till we got outside. Go for it when he opened the trunk.

Suddenly Razor shoved me to the left, toward the walk-in. "In here," he said.

My stomach lurched. "But I thought—"

"Just for a minute while I pull the car up to the back door."

Panic rushed through me. He was going to lock me in the walk-in. Sneider's dead body flashed through my head. Was that the plan? Was he going to stab me and leave my body in the walk-in?

I tried to slow down, but the tip of the knife jabbed me in the back. I felt a trickle of blood seep down my spine.

"Keep up, Oz," he said. He swung open the walk-in door with his free hand. A blast of cold air hit me.

"*Oz?* What . . . ?"

Razor and I turned at the same time. Neither one of us had heard the door open.

It was Rusty. She was standing at the back door with the spare key dangling from her finger. She was smiling, happy to see us.

"Rusty—get out!"

Her eyes darted from me to Razor. She moved but too late. Razor dove toward her. I tried to free my hands, but the plastic wrap was too tight. I threw my whole body at Razor. I smashed into his back, throwing us both to the floor. I had him pinned down. But he was too strong. I couldn't hold him for long.

"*RUSTY, GET—*" I looked up. The back door was empty. Rusty was gone.

CHAPTER LII

The back door wasn't empty for long. In a split second, cops burst through the door. One of them lifted me off the floor and half carried me out of the kitchen. I managed to glance back once. Razor was on the floor, spread-eagle, surrounded by police. Next thing I knew, I was in the parking lot. Someone cut the plastic off my hands. I leaned against the wall, trying to stop shaking. Where was Rusty? The sun blinded me for a second but then I saw her, over by a police car. Safe.

I ran over. "You okay?" I asked, trying to catch my breath.

She nodded. "Yeah. Good thing the cops were here."

"How *did* they get here?"

"I called them," she said.

"You *called* them?"

A sheepish smile crept over her face. "I copied Suarez's number off the card he gave you when you weren't looking."

"You went through my stuff?" I said. "I can't believe you went through my stuff."

"Hello? I just saved your life, didn't I?"

"How about I saved *your* life? Besides, I was here looking for you."

"How did you figure that?"

"I found the pad of paper with the note written on it. 'Go back to the scene of the crime.' So I figured . . ."

She scrunched her eyes together. "The *original* scene of the crime. I went to Los Alamos. I decided to hitch a ride with my parents after all."

"But this morning . . . you rode off . . . I thought . . ."

She shook her head. "I needed to burn off some steam. I was mad, really mad."

"Yeah, I got that. But Los Alamos?"

"I thought I'd dig around . . . see what I could find out about Harrison Smith, your dad, Powell—all of them."

"And?"

She smirked, clearly pleased with herself. "So I went to the library up there."

"That's why I couldn't get you on your cell phone?"

She nodded. "Look what I found," she said. She pulled out a black-and-white photocopy from her bag.

"What is it?"

"An article from a Los Alamos employee newsletter. Look at the photo."

It was the picture of my dad that we'd found in Sneider's motel room. I looked at the byline. "Harrison Smith? He wrote this?"

"Yeah, and took the picture. See the credit? It's all about this crack team of physicists he'd put together: your dad, Victor Martinez, and A. J. Powell. So I wondered why he never mentioned that he was your dad's boss."

"Convenient amnesia."

"Exactly," she said. "So when I couldn't reach you, I freaked. I figured you were with Harrison and I . . ." She didn't finish. She hesitated for a moment, then looked over at me. "I thought Harrison had killed you. I thought you were dead." Neither one of us said anything.

I cleared my throat and looked away. Rusty did too. "So I called Detective Suarez. He told me what had happened and said you were MIA."

"How did you figure out I was at Chez Isabelle?"

"You're always at Chez Isabelle," she said, smiling.

"Good thing she did." It was Suarez. "You're a hard man to track down," he said, walking over to us.

"I—I'm sorry about that." I was trying to think of something to say that didn't sound totally lame when his phone rang.

Suarez took the call. "You're there now? Good." He paused, listening. "No charges right now. Just tell Mrs. Martinez that we'd like her to come in to answer some questions."

Rusty and I looked at each other. *Mrs. Martinez— Linda Martinez?*

"Tell her I've spoken with her attorney." Suarez shifted the phone and nodded. "Yep. Let her know that Mr. McCallister told us she's willing to make a full statement detailing everything she knows about her husband's murder."

Rusty and I shot each other another look. *McCallister? Archie McCallister?* Archie was Linda Martinez's lawyer? Was that what he was doing at her house?

Suarez hung up and turned back to us. "You two okay?"

"Is Archie really Linda Martinez's lawyer?" I blurted out.

"Yes. Why?" he asked.

I wasn't sure. I tried to sort it out in my head. "I . . . I . . ."

"Look, slow down. It sounds like Mrs. Martinez panicked after Sneider visited her. She was afraid he'd figure out that she'd covered up her husband's murder. So she decided it was time to talk to a lawyer."

"So she called Archie," Rusty put in.

"Exactly," said Suarez.

"But if she told Archie what happened, why didn't he say anything?" I asked.

"Because she hadn't told him anything yet. She said she was in trouble but wouldn't say more. I figure she was hoping she could make a deal."

"So Archie wasn't involved with Mrs. Martinez or Harrison?"

"No," said Suarez, smiling. "He was on your side."

Rusty shot me a look. I knew what it meant. It was as good a time as any. "Detective Suarez . . . about this afternoon," I said. "I'm sorry about the vanishing act."

He held his hand up. "Save it. It's been a long day; we'll talk later. But I've got some good news. I thought you'd like to know that your brother is being released."

"That's great. Thanks," I said. "Thanks for everything."

"Don't thank me. You guys figured it out." He smiled and walked past us into the restaurant. I couldn't believe it. Dave was free. I felt free too, like finally everything was going to be okay.

Rusty was beaming. I tried to think of something to say. I had to thank her. "Rusty, I—I couldn't—"

She smiled. "I know . . . you don't have to say anything."

"But—," I mumbled.

She reached out and touched my arm. She smiled. "Like Suarez said, save it."

"I was sure Dad was innocent," I said. Dave and I were in his office. He looked up from a pile of paperwork.

"And I was sure he was guilty," he said. He leaned back in his desk chair and stretched. "Who knows? Maybe we were both right."

"How do you figure *that*?" I asked. I twirled a pencil on top of his desk and watched it spin.

Dave shrugged. "Harrison told you Dad changed his mind. Dad was going to steal classified documents, but in the end he didn't do it. That's the important thing, isn't it?"

"Yeah, maybe."

Dave nodded. "I'm not saying Dad was squeaky clean.

He made a mistake. He wasn't perfect, but I can deal with that. Can you?"

I looked up at Dave. I wasn't sure. I didn't say anything. Maybe he was right. Maybe I'd have to live with a dad who wasn't a hero but wasn't a traitor, either.

"There's one thing I don't get," I said.

Dave signed the bottom of an invoice and glanced over at me. "What's that?"

"The night Sneider was murdered . . . where were you?"

He sighed. "I was afraid you were going to ask that." He set the pen down. He paused and then said, "I went to find Sneider."

I sat up straight and slammed my hand down on top of the spinning pencil. "You *what*?"

"Oz, cool it, okay? Let me explain." He got up and shut the door to his office.

"I can't believe you—"

Dave interrupted me. "I never found him."

"I don't—"

"I saw his name in the reservations book. At first I figured it was some other Aaron Sneider—just some weird coincidence. But in the back of my mind I think I knew it was him. I found a photo of Sneider on the Internet, so when he walked in that night I knew it was him."

"So what did you do?"

"I panicked. I figured he had to be here because of the story he'd written. I freaked out that it was all going to come out again."

"Yeah? And then?"

"Then I got angry. He'd blown my life apart before, and now he was going to do it again. I figured the local number he'd given for his dinner reservation must be a hotel. I called and got his room number. I decided to go there after I closed the restaurant."

"What? And make him say he was sorry?"

Dave shook his head. "Okay, I deserve that. It was stupid, I know that now. But all I wanted was for him to leave us alone. Luckily, Carlos stopped me."

"So Carlos *was* involved?"

"Sort of. He saw that I was ballistic. I ended up telling him the whole story. He tried to get me to change my mind. When I wouldn't, he insisted on coming with me. If he hadn't and I'd found Sneider, I'm not sure what would have happened."

"So you and Carlos drove to the motel?" I said.

"Yeah. I pounded on the door, but no one answered."

"Yeah, because Sneider was at the restaurant thinking he was meeting you." My head was swirling. I couldn't believe what Dave was telling me.

"So what did you do?"

He grimaced. "So then I got *really* angry and punched a column at the motel."

"You punched one of those concrete columns?" I couldn't help smiling. "You're lucky you didn't break every bone in your hand."

"Felt like I did. Carlos took me to his place and bandaged my hand. It was late and I was still mental, so he convinced me to crash on his couch."

"So why didn't you tell the cops?"

"You're joking, aren't you? They already thought I was guilty, so a late-night visit to the murder victim hardly would have helped. Besides, I had to protect Carlos."

"Protect him? From what?"

"Carlos is about to get his green card. Any day now. The last thing he needs is the cops thinking he's involved in a murder. He couldn't risk it. I told him to clear out for a few days until things died down."

"Only they didn't . . ."

Dave grimaced. "Only they didn't."

A knock at the door stopped me from saying anything else.

"Come in," said Dave.

JoJo poked his head in. "Welcome back, Dave. We still on for tonight?"

"Absolutely."

JoJo gave a broad grin. "Excellent. I'll get the front of house ready."

As he closed the door, I said, "Are you sure you want to do this?"

"We've got to sometime," said Dave.

"Yeah, I know, but . . ." Even as I said it, I knew Dave was right. We had to reopen as soon as possible. We'd called the staff and asked them to come in for a family meal. A couple of the guys had come in early to pitch in.

To be honest, it wasn't tonight I was worried about. Tonight was just a way to say thanks. Rusty and her mom and dad were coming. Archie was picking Mom up at the airport so they'd be here. With a handful of others we'd have a full house.

"Do you think anyone will show? I mean tomorrow, when we open for real," I asked. Might as well say it. I knew Dave was thinking the same thing as me.

Dave was quiet for a minute, thinking. Finally he shrugged and smiled. "We'll see," he said. It was the first time I'd seen him smile in a long time. He looked tired, but there was something else. He looked happy.

"Heard you did a pretty good job cooking the other night," he said.

I felt my face go hot. "I helped out, you know . . ." My voice petered out.

"I heard it was more than that. I could use your help tonight, if you're up for it."

I looked over at him, searching his face. He wasn't kidding. He meant it.

I didn't say anything. Finally Dave stood up. "See you in the kitchen?"

"Yeah. I'll be with you in a sec, okay?"

"Sure. Take your time."

I kept thinking about what Dave had said about Dad. Maybe he wasn't as innocent as I'd hoped. But he wasn't as guilty as everyone thought he was either. It was time to set the record straight.

I unzipped my backpack and dug around until I found the two things I needed. The first was a telephone number. I punched it in. Hopefully he was still there. The receptionist answered and put me through. He picked up on the first ring.

"Jake Whitetower, *Particle* magazine."

I explained who I was—who I *really* was—and said, "Remember the story you were working on about Aaron

Sneider's murder? Well I think I've got a bigger scoop for you...."

I told Jake the story about Harrison, Powell, my dad, and Victor Martinez. While we were talking, I picked up the second thing I'd pulled out of my backpack. It was the sage smudge stick Rusty's mom had given me. I lit one end and watched a small plume of smoke drift up. I breathed in the smell of burning herbs and glanced around me. What was it she had said? Something about how it would rid Chez Isabelle of all negativity.

It already has, I thought. It already has.

ACKNOWLEDGMENTS

Thanks to Jayne Reich, Lucie Roberts, Alison Catchpole and especially Sophie McKenzie for helping me turn my "what if . . . ?" into a story. My agents Jill Hughes and Gina Maccoby offered sage advice, support, and encouragement. Alyson Heller and Liesa Abrams deftly guided me through the editing process and made the book much, much better.

Special thanks to Zach and my mom, who read the book countless times and were constant champions. And to my grandmother Mary Pace, who called Santa Fe home.